Halloween Hue-Dunit

Paula Darnell

Campbell and Rogers Press

CR

Campbell and Rogers Press

This is a work of fiction. Characters, names, events, places, incidents, business establishments, and organizations portrayed in this novel are the product of the author's imagination or are used fictitiously.

ISBN: 978-1-887402-42-2

Cover design by Molly Burton with Cozy Cover Designs

First Edition

Published by Campbell and Rogers Press

https://www.campbellandrogerspress.com

Dedicated, with love,
to my family –
Gary, Andrea and Dan, Sara and Jason,
George and Gerianne

Chapter 1

"Dahlings, I'm ba-a-ack!" announced the blonde woman in a throaty voice.

When she appeared, Pamela, the director of the Roadrunner, our co-op art gallery, had just called our semi-annual meeting to order.

As the member artists turned toward the door of our meeting room to see who had spoken, Frank, one of our board members, rushed to her and gave her a big hug. By the time they'd untangled, every other man in the room had gathered around her to make the same move.

It didn't escape my notice that none of the women had done the same. In fact, many of them had distinctly sour expressions on their faces. Obviously, they knew who she was, but I didn't have a clue. I'd joined the Roadrunner about a year and a half earlier, shortly after I'd moved to Lonesome Valley to pursue a career as a full-time artist after my husband had divorced me so that he'd be free to marry a young woman barely older than our college-age daughter Emma, so our visitor must have been from before my time.

I turned to my friend Susan, who was sitting at the table next to me. "Who is she?"

"Monique d'Albert. She used to be a member here. When she married, she moved to Palm Springs, and, as far as I know, nobody here has heard from her since, until today. Maybe she's visiting. I sure hope she's not moving back."

Susan glanced at the interloper with distaste.

"Why do you say that?"

"Well, just look. Every man she comes into contact with goes ga-ga, and she plays it to the hilt. Evidently, no man is immune to her charms. That's how she wound up married to a ninety-year-old multi-million-aire."

"A gold-digger, huh?"

"Exactly. I *will* give her this, though. She's an excellent artist. In fact, she's fairly well known for her pastels."

"Members! Please! Let's come to order now and get down to business," Pamela said, banging her gavel for emphasis. "We have a short list of agenda items, which won't take long to cover."

By this point, Frank had found Monique a chair in the front of the room. Solicitously, he pulled it out from beneath a table and made sure that she was seated comfortably.

Pamela glanced pointedly at Frank.

"Go ahead, Pamela. Don't mind me. I'll just grab a cup of coffee for Monique."

He headed for the back of the room, where a large coffee urn had been set up. His actions earned him a glare from his wife Valerie, and when he returned to his seat next to her after delivering a Styrofoam cup of coffee to Monique, Valerie turned her back on him. Considering the couple had been married only a few months, although they'd known each other for years, I wasn't too surprised by Valerie's reaction.

In the meantime, Pamela ignored his suggestion, waiting until Frank was seated before she began. By this time, everyone had quieted down, and she didn't need to raise her voice to be heard.

"Before we get to our first order of business, I'd like to welcome our former member back to the Roadrunner. Are you in town visiting, Monique?"

"Oh, no! I'm back to stay. Unfortunately, my husband passed away last month, and I just couldn't bear to stay in our home in Palm Springs without him."

"I'm so sorry to hear that, Monique," Pamela said pensively. I knew she was thinking about her own husband who'd died three months earlier. It was bad enough that Pamela had lost Rich, but the way she'd lost him was horrible, too. He'd been murdered, and now his killer was awaiting trial in the county jail.

Carrie, the red-haired jewelry artist who was sitting next to Monique, leaned over and whispered something to her. Monique nodded.

"Thank you, Pamela," she said simply, "and I'm awfully sorry to hear about Rich. He was such a nice guy."

When a shadow passed over Pamela's face, I surmised that Monique had probably flirted with Rich when she'd been a member of the Roadrunner previously. Although our gallery director probably didn't especially appreciate Monique's comment, she politely acknowledged it before Monique piped up again.

"Since I'll be moving back here to Lonesome Valley, I'd like to renew my membership in the Roadrunner."

"Yes, of course, since you were a member in good standing when you left, reinstatement is automatic, but I'm afraid we don't have space in the gallery right now."

"She can have mine," Chip immediately volunteered. "I'll be working on some murals for the Downtown Merchants' Association for the next few months, anyway."

I had a feeling that if Chip hadn't offered to give up his space, one of the other men would have. Although Susan's nephew Chip was a talented artist, he didn't seem to be able to find a path forward in his art career, perhaps because he often lacked follow-through and he worked at his father's pizza parlor to make ends meet. Giving up his wall space probably wasn't as big a deal for him as it would have been for some of the other artists because he often didn't fill his space, anyway.

Well aware of Chip's propensities, Pamela agreed to the arrangement and then began to talk about the first agenda item, a Saturday class in pumpkin painting for elementary school students. Although I had no teaching experience whatsoever, I'd agreed to help with the class. I understood that I'd be giving a short demo and then circulating to help any kids who had questions, so it wasn't as though I'd really be teaching. Valerie and Frank, both high school art teachers, would be leading the class. Despite that, I felt a bit nervous about my demo, probably because the idea of public speaking had always terrified me.

As Pamela continued to tick off items on the meeting agenda, Chip caught Monique's eye and winked at her. She smiled at him, and, encouraged, he proceeded to wiggle his eyebrows and cross his eyes, eliciting giggles from Monique and a frown from Pamela.

After that, Chip grabbed his copy of the agenda and didn't look back up until Pamela declared the meeting adjourned. Instead of rushing to Monique as the rest of the men did, Chip hung back and spoke to Pamela. They were friends, and I suspected he regretted his actions if they'd caused Pamela any grief, although what he did was entirely in character for him since he was quite the flirt himself, as Pamela well knew from past experience.

Susan and I followed the other members into the gallery, where Monique was holding court with the men. When Valerie tugged at her husband's elbow in an effort to get his attention, he barely glanced at her before turning back to Monique.

Valerie tapped Frank's arm once more and announced that she was leaving, and he could find his own way home. *That* got his attention, but Valerie was already out the door before he could stop her. By this time, everyone was staring at Frank, but he shrugged and pasted a weak smile on his face.

Meanwhile, Pamela had emerged from the meeting room.

"Monique, let's go back to my office, and we can get your paperwork filled out now."

"Great!" Monique turned to her fans and said, "Au revoir, mes amis."

"Huh? What did she just say?" Lonnie asked.

"Did you forget your high school French?" Heather, his wife, asked.

"I never learned it in the first place. I flunked French, remember?"

Heather just laughed. It was pretty clear that she *did* remember.

"She said 'goodbye, my friends.'"

"Oh, OK. How come she didn't say it in English?"

"She comes from the French aristocracy, doesn't she?" Frank asked. "I think she may be a duchess or something."

Susan smirked at this assertion. "Sure she is," she whispered to me, "and I'm the queen of England."

The crowd began to disperse, although a few members hung around for a while, chatting.

Pamela and Monique came back into the gallery about five minutes later. The contrast between the two women couldn't have been more noticeable. Tiny Pamela stood less than five feet tall, and she wore a beige pantsuit that was a bit too loose on her. I'd never understood why she preferred to wear beige, tan, or brown because those hues weren't very flattering on her. Monique, on the other hand, was probably at least eight inches taller than Pamela, and she stood out in a Chanel suit, the latest from Paris, if I didn't miss my guess. I was sure I'd seen the exact same black and white tweed suit in the September issue of *Vogue*. My dear friend and next-door neighbor Belle had a subscription, and the current issue was always sitting on her coffee table. Besides her designer suit, Monique carried a burgundy Lady Dior handbag and sported a large pink topaz ring, set in white gold or perhaps platinum, on her right hand, but her left hand was devoid of jewelry with no wedding or engagement ring in sight. Her ensemble had obviously cost a small fortune, but that shouldn't have come as a surprise since her husband had been quite wealthy. Now, I supposed, Monique was the wealthy one.

"Why do you think Monique wants to come back to the Roadrunner?" I asked Susan. "She's definitely no starving artist."

"I don't know. It does seem a little odd. To tell you the truth, she seemed to be really happy to be leaving Lonesome Valley two years ago. I remember that, at the time, one of the members told her she'd have to be sure to come back to see us sometime, and she said she didn't think that was ever going to happen."

A tapping at the Roadrunner's front door caught our attention. The gallery closed at five, but since all the lights were on, it was obvious that people were inside. The gray-haired woman outside continued to knock on the door, even after Frank shook his head and mouthed "we're closed." Finally, Chip opened the door a crack to give her the message up close and personal, but when she stuck her foot in the door, Chip stepped back and she barged into the gallery.

Her unexpected move had caught Chip off guard, and he stared at her in surprise.

"Sorry about that, son," she said.

Now that I could see her more clearly, her wrinkled face made me think that she was probably in her late sixties, perhaps older.

"I'm looking for Monique Dee Albert," she announced.

"It's pronounced Doll Bear," Monique, who'd just come back into the gallery with Pamela, informed her. "Monique Doll Bear," she repeated.

"Whatever," the woman said dismissively. "I'm an investigator, and I have some questions for you."

"Let's see some identification," Frank demanded.

The woman pulled a wallet out of the pocket of her jeans jacket as Frank approached her. When he came closer, she snatched it away. "No you don't," she told him. "I'll show it to Ms. Dee Albert."

"Doll Bear," Monique corrected with a sigh. She peered at the identification card and burst out laughing.

"You're not a detective!"

"Never said I was. I'm a private investigator."

"I have no intention of talking to you."

"Wouldn't you like to clear your name?"

"Don't be ridiculous. I don't know what you're talking about."

"Sure you do, honey, and pretty soon all these good people will know, too."

"Are you threatening me?"

"Just stating a fact, Ms. Dee Albert."

"I think it's time you left," Frank said, unsuccessfully attempting to take the PI's arm so that he could guide her to the door.

"You heard the man," Chip said. "Get lost!"

"OK, OK. I'm going, but you haven't heard the last of me, Ms. Dee Albert. I'll be watching your every move." With that, she turned and exited the Roadrunner.

Frank and Chip immediately rushed to Monique, but she assured them that she was fine. Nobody dared ask her what the private investigator had been referring to.

"I think I'll be getting back to my cousin's house now. She'll be expecting me," Monique said.

"Let me drive you," Chip offered.

"Well, isn't that sweet of you, Chip, but I have my ride here," she said, reaching into her designer bag and plucking out her keys.

"Well, the least I can do is walk you to your car, then." Chip offered her his arm, and she clung to it as they left the gallery.

"Wait up!" Frank called. "I'll come with you."

Chapter 2

I headed home to less drama. My golden retriever Laddie was waiting for me by the kitchen door, and Mona Lisa, my persnickety calico cat, even showed up to welcome me home. While Laddie bounced up and down, his tail twirling in the air, Mona Lisa executed a figure eight by winding around my ankles. Laddie didn't leave my side as I deposited my keys in the little china bowl on the kitchen counter, but Mona Lisa scampered off to lie beside my daughter Emma, who was sitting on the couch reading a textbook.

My six-hundred-square-foot house was small, but cozy. Emma was staying with me since she'd transferred from college in California to Northern Arizona University. With two people and two pets, it could be a tight fit at times, but we managed.

It helped that my attached art studio was the same size as the house, so I had plenty of room there for my paintings, and since it had a separate outside door, the space worked perfectly as a stop on Lonesome Valley's weekly studio tour, which took place every Friday, except for a couple of months in the winter.

"Hi, Mom, how was the meeting?" Emma asked, setting her book aside.

"Livelier than usual." I told Emma about Monique's arrival, how all the men had reacted to her, and that Valerie had left Frank to find his own way home.

"I don't blame her," Emma said. "If Matt ever pulled something like that, I'd be furious, too."

Emma had been dating her boyfriend Matt for several months now. They'd met at the feed store where Matt was assistant manager. Belle's husband Dennis managed the store, and it was thanks to him that Emma had been able to work there part-time whenever she had a break from college. Now that she'd transferred to NAU, she worked in the store twenty or thirty hours a week, but Matt, who was also attending NAU, continued to work full-time, putting in forty or fifty hours most weeks.

"You're not going out with Matt tonight?"

"No, I have to study for a history test."

"I'm sure you'll do fine."

Emma had always been serious about her studies, and she was a good student.

"I hope so. I'll be glad when it's over, anyway."

Leaving Emma to her studies, I went outside with Laddie and stood on the patio while he wandered around the backyard for a while, and then we went to bed.

It seemed as though I'd just fallen asleep when my affable retriever began nudging my arm with his nose. I glanced at the bedside clock and saw that it was already six o'clock. Laddie wanted to go for his morning walk.

I groaned and rolled out of bed, but, by the time I'd dressed, I was wide awake. Emma was restoring the hide-a-bed to its sofa position when I went to the kitchen to get Laddie's leash. Since my small home had only one bedroom, I'd offered to subdivide the studio so that Emma could have her own room when she decided to stay with me while attending NAU, but she insisted on sleeping on the hide-a-bed.

"Good luck with your test," I said, as she pulled on her jacket and grabbed her backpack.

"Thanks, Mom." She parted the curtain and looked outside. "Here's Matt now. Gotta go. I'll see you later."

Mona Lisa emitted a plaintive meow and leaped to the top of her kitty tree. She favored Emma over Laddie and me, and she wasted no time turning her back on us.

Unconcerned with his feline roommate's snub, Laddie pranced impatiently until I brought out his collar and leash, and then he stood still while I put them on him. Without further ado, we were out the door and on our way to the nearby park where we usually walked in the morning. Our walk turned out to be uneventful.

When we returned home, Mona Lisa was waiting at the door and wasted no time pouncing on my feet. I got the message: she wanted breakfast, and she wanted it *now*.

"Sorry, Mona Lisa," I told her. "You're going to have to wait a while."

I knew she'd understood exactly what I'd said when she turned in a huff and launched herself to the top of her kitty tree.

Laddie put his paw on my leg and looked up at me.

"Here you go, Laddie," I said, taking off his collar and leash.

While my golden boy flopped down on the floor, I stepped into the kitchen, trying to decide whether I'd start my morning with tea or coffee. Tea had been my go-to morning drink for years, but lately

I'd favored coffee more often than not. I'd developed a taste for coffee drinks since I almost always had one from the Coffee Klatsch next door to the Roadrunner when I did my required floor duty. All members worked two days a month in the gallery. When possible, I opted to work four half days. This morning happened to be one of those half days. Since I'd be at the gallery from nine to one and I'd undoubtedly be enjoying a mocha, I decided on tea to start the day.

After I'd had a couple of cups and my golden boy had cooled down from our walk, I fed Laddie and Mona Lisa and fixed myself a bowl of cereal. I had plenty of time before I had to get ready to go to the Roadrunner, and I puttered around, checking email on my cell phone while watching the morning news on television.

Distracted as I was by multi-tasking, I almost missed seeing Monique's face plastered on the screen. According to the announcer, Monique and her late husband's daughter were in a bitter feud over the multi-millionaire's estate. After the death of famous industrialist Edward McCall, Monique had produced a will naming her sole heir, cutting McCall's daughter out of any inheritance. McCall's lawyer had had a different will, which didn't include Monique. Now each woman would be seeking to have the court decide in her favor.

I was tempted to call Susan to tell her what I'd just heard, but since she was also scheduled to work in the gallery, I decided to wait to talk to her later. As I showered and dressed, I wondered whether we'd be seeing any more of Monique, now that her problems had been plastered all over the national news.

My question was answered soon after I arrived at the gallery. Pamela had just unlocked the door for Susan and me when Monique pulled up and parked in front of the gallery. She gave us a cheerful wave before opening her trunk and struggling to pull a large box out.

"Hold up, Monique!" Chip shouted from across the street. "I'll get that for you."

He jogged over and lifted the box while Monique closed the trunk.

"Thank you soooo much, Chip!" she said, batting her eyes.

"No problem at all," he replied.

I couldn't help noticing that Pamela rolled her eyes at the exchange, but she didn't hang around to watch the pair. Susan set up the cash register while I did some light dusting to prepare the gallery for opening and Pamela retreated to her office.

In the meantime, Chip removed his paintings from his designated area on the back wall while Monique looked on, all the while engaging him in flirtatious banter, which wasn't difficult because flirting came as naturally as breathing to Chip.

When I finished dusting, I unlocked the gallery door, although there were no potential customers waiting outside and I anticipated a fairly quiet morning.

When Chip began hauling his paintings upstairs to his studio, Monique walked around the gallery looking at other members' displays. She didn't make a move to unpack her box or come over to the cash wrap to chat with Susan and me.

After dashing up the stairs with his paintings and back down several times, Chip finally finished his task and joined Monique in the back area of the gallery. He was barely out of breath. If I'd run up and down the stairs as he had, I'd have been panting for sure, and that's assuming I'd have the stamina to keep it up. Of course, he was twenty-six to my fifty-one, so that probably helped.

While Susan re-arranged some jewelry in the glass display case next to the cash register, I peeked in the back to see what was going on. While Monique stood back, Chip took her paintings out of the box and set them against the wall. Then, Monique directed him on their placement as he hung each painting.

My curiosity got the better of me, and I joined them to look at Monique's work. Each piece was a small pastel, exquisitely framed under glass. Although oil painting was my specialty and I'd never worked in pastels except briefly during college studio art classes, I could appreciate and admire her talent.

"Monique, what a beautiful display! Your artwork's fantastic."

"Oh, do you really think so?"

"Of course."

"So do I," Chip piped up. "It's amazing!"

"You're so sweet," Monique said softly, gazing up at Chip. Then, she reached over and touched my arm. "You, too, honey."

Just then the little bell on the gallery door tinkled, alerting us to the arrival of a potential customer. I walked around the partition that partially obscured the back area of the gallery so that I could greet the new arrival, but Susan beat me to it.

Wearing a jeans jacket over a print dress and sporting Western boots, the thirty-something woman had a storm-cloud look on her face.

"May I help you?" Susan asked.

"I'm looking for Monique d'Albert," she announced. "Is she here?"

"Yes, in the back. Just around the partition there," Susan told her.

"Thanks."

Susan and I exchanged a glance as the woman walked purposefully to the back of the gallery. I still hadn't had a chance to ask Susan whether or not she'd heard this morning's news report about Monique, especially since I didn't want to take a chance on Monique's overhearing our conversation.

"Hi, Faye, I didn't know you planned to come to the gallery this morning," Monique said. "I'd like you to meet Chip. He's been terribly helpful, arranging all my artwork. Chip, this is my cousin Faye."

Chip grinned and stuck his hand out to shake Faye's, but she ignored him.

"Just what do you think you're doing, cozying up to Grant?" she demanded. "He was practically slobbering all over you at breakfast this morning."

"Why, whatever do you mean?"

"You know *exactly* what I mean. You haven't changed a bit! I don't know what I was thinking—agreeing to let you stay with us, but I want you to leave. Work your wiles on somebody else's husband or on this guy here. I don't care! Just leave Grant alone! He's *my* husband!"

Faye turned and stalked out of the Roadrunner, and we all stood there in stunned silence. However, Faye wasn't done yet. After a few seconds, she returned with a suitcase and flung it inside.

Horrified, Monique ran to the bag that her cousin had just unceremoniously dumped on the gallery floor and put her arms around it.

"Oh, no! My Louis Vuitton!"

Chapter 3

Cradling her "baby," Monique wrapped her arms around the suitcase. After several seconds, she paused to examine it closely.

"I don't think there's any damage," Chip assured her, as he stooped to look at the bag. Extending his hand, he helped her up.

"Faye's always been so hateful to me, and I've never done a *thing* to deserve it," she murmured. "Now, I need to find someplace else to stay."

"Problem solved," Chip told her. "You can stay right here."

Monique looked at him in confusion. "What do you mean?"

"You can stay in the apartment upstairs. It's on loan to me, but I'm not living there. I only use the second-floor studio across the hall from the apartment."

"*Really?*" Monique asked breathlessly.

"Really," Chip assured her. "I can take your suitcase upstairs right now."

An awkward silence ensued while Chip carried Monique's bag to the second-floor apartment.

Pamela had heard the commotion and joined us in the gallery, but Monique avoided looking our way, as she dug in her purse and came up with her car keys.

As soon as Chip returned, Monique dangled her keys and told him that she had a few more things in the trunk.

"Say no more. I'll bring everything in," Chip said, taking her keys.

We all waited as he ran upstairs with two more pieces of Louis Vuitton luggage and bounced back down, taking the steps two at a time.

"All set."

"Chip, you're such a lifesaver," Monique cooed, taking his arm.

"You've had a tough morning already, and it's only just past nine. Let's go next door for coffee."

"All right, sugar."

As they exited the Roadrunner, Chip turned toward us with a silly grin on his face and winked.

"Oh, brother," Susan sighed. "I hope my nephew knows what he's doing."

"I'm not crazy about her living upstairs," Pamela said, "but the apartment's his, and he can do what he likes with it, so I can't prevent him from letting Monique stay there. I guess I'll have to provide her with a key to the gallery. I just hope she's not careless about locking the door."

"I wonder why she took Chip up on his offer," Susan said. "Surely she can afford to stay at the Lonesome Valley Resort."

"Didn't she used to date Brooks? Maybe she doesn't want to see him," Pamela replied.

Brooks Miller, the manager of the Resort, was a failed artist who'd once had his own gallery not far from the Roadrunner, but he'd closed it in favor of opening a gallery at the Resort, where he featured famous artists. He was also a very wealthy man. It was rumored that his family was the richest in the entire state.

"Maybe that's it," Susan agreed.

"Or maybe she can't afford to stay there," I said before reporting what I'd heard on the morning news.

We couldn't discuss Monique's situation any further because a couple with two small children came into the gallery. While Pamela showed them around, Susan and I tried to keep the kids occupied in the meeting room by showing them how to draw faces on some tiny pumpkins.

When their parents were ready to leave, we gave the kids their pumpkins to take home with them.

"Oh, how cute!" their mother exclaimed, as they held their painted pumpkins up to show her.

"Let me pay for those," their father said, reaching for his wallet.

"No need," Pamela told him. "They're on the house, and thank you for your purchase."

The man held a small paper bag in his hand. I waited until the couple and their children left the gallery before I asked Pamela what they had bought.

"One of Monique's pastels."

"That was quick," Susan said. "They haven't been hanging there more than a few minutes."

"Yes, I think she'll do very well here again. Her artwork was always very popular," Pamela said. "Unfortunately, trouble seems to follow her wherever she goes, and she brings some of it on herself."

"I doubt that her legal problems will be resolved anytime soon. The fight over her late husband's estate could take years to resolve," I observed.

Our gossip session was interrupted when another visitor came into the gallery, this time not a customer, but one of our members.

"Hi, Carrie." Pamela did a double take. "You've cut your hair! It looks great."

"Do you really think so?"

"Yes, I do."

"It's very flattering," I said.

"I agree," Susan added. "That short, wavy style suits you perfectly."

Carrie smiled. "I really wasn't sure about it, but I think I like it, too."

Carrie had kept her auburn hair long ever since I'd first met her. Judging by its length, I knew that she'd let it grow for years. Unfortunately, she was a bit plump, and her long tresses had had the effect of emphasizing her extra pounds; whereas her new style showcased her face, rather than her figure.

"I rearranged the jewelry display because some of your pieces sold, and the top shelf was looking a little empty," Susan told Carrie.

"Thanks, Susan. I brought a few more necklaces and a couple of display busts we can put on top of the counter if it's all right with you, Pamela."

"That sounds fine. Let's see what you've made."

We gathered around the counter while Carrie unbagged her turquoise jewelry and showed it to us.

"The stones are from the Kingman turquoise mine. I usually go there to source a couple of times a year."

"Beautiful," I said as I lifted one of the necklaces and put it on a display bust that Carrie placed on the top of the counter. "Someone will be very happy to buy this." What I didn't say was that I was tempted to buy it myself, but I needed to stick to my budget. Just as I felt I couldn't afford to buy my own paintings, the same caveat applied to most of the other members' artwork.

"Thanks, Amanda. By the way, I wanted to ask you and Susan if you've decided what you're going to wear for my costume party."

"Costume party?"

We turned just as the tinkling bell signaled someone's arrival—in this case, Monique's.

"Costume party!" she repeated. "Count me in!"

Chapter 4

"Hello, Monique," Carrie greeted her. "Of course, you're invited. The party's this Saturday night at seven at my house. I sent invitations to all the members of the Roadrunner, but that was before you came back to town and rejoined us."

"Ooh, marvelous!" She turned to Chip, who had followed her into the Roadrunner. "You'll go with me, won't you, Chip?" Without waiting for him to answer, she declared, "I'd just *love* to have a handsome date for the party."

"Sure, my pleasure," Chip replied with a wide grin.

"This will be such fun! Now, I need to decide on a costume."

Pamela, who'd been observing their interaction, turned and walked back to her office, leaving the rest of us to discuss the upcoming event. I knew Pamela wasn't planning on attending. Since her husband's death, she'd put in long hours at the gallery and hadn't done much painting, although she'd resumed holding open studio as a stop on Lonesome Valley's weekly art studio tour a few weeks after Rich's death. It didn't help that his business had been in crisis at the time, and Pamela was still dealing with his company's ongoing problems. The members of the Roadrunner were trying their best to support her, but we couldn't solve her problems or even buoy her spirits most days. She and Chip were friends, and he was usually sensitive to her feelings, but Monique's arrival had his full attention now, and he didn't pay any attention when Pamela left the room.

We all noticed when Lieutenant Belmont showed up at the Road-runner's door, though. As soon as she saw the grumpy detective, Susan ducked behind the counter, grabbing a large binder from the drawer below and pretending to study it.

I couldn't help observing that the lieutenant wore a nicely tailored sports coat and coordinating tie, rather than his usual ill-fitting, rumpled suit. Maybe he was turning over a new leaf; he'd certainly never bothered to make an effort where his appearance was concerned before now.

"Is Mrs. Smith in?" he asked Carrie.

"Yes, she's in her office," Carrie said. "Would you like me to take you back?"

"I know the way," he said.

He hadn't spoken a word to me although normally he would have made some sarcastic comment. The lieutenant and I had a bit of a checkered history. He'd given me a hard time during some of his cases, but we'd also worked together in a couple of instances, and I believed he had a grudging respect for me, despite his usual rudeness. On the other hand, Susan despised the man because he'd arrested her for a murder someone else had committed and she'd spent a horrible night in the local jail before being released the following day. It was no wonder she was avoiding him now.

The lieutenant nodded to me and went on back to Pamela's office. Her door was open, and he didn't close it behind him when he went in.

We could hear their voices in quiet discussion, but we couldn't make out what they said.

"Who was that guy?" Monique asked.

"Nobody you want to know," Chip told her. "He's a police detective and a nasty dude."

Monique frowned for an instant before pasting on her happy face again. "Let's go up to the apartment, and I'll find my extra set of keys," Chip suggested, and the two wasted no time going upstairs.

In the meantime, Susan slipped into the meeting room to avoid seeing Lieutenant Belmont, leaving Carrie and me alone in the gallery.

"What do you suppose he's doing here?" Carrie asked.

"No idea. Possibly something about the upcoming trial."

"I guess. Have you decided on your costume for the party yet?"

"Yes. My friend Belle's making it for me. I can't sew a stitch, but she's an expert. She came up with the idea."

"Is it going to be a surprise?"

"No, not really. It's a Victorian bathing suit. Believe me, it doesn't look anything like what you'd see on a beach today."

"I can imagine."

"I'm pretty much going to be covered head to toe. The Victorians liked to wear lots of clothing! Belle remembered seeing a Folkwear pattern for it. She volunteered to sew the costume for me, and I thought it might be cute, so I ordered it. I'm supposed to have a fitting this afternoon."

"I can't wait to see it. Is your boyfriend going to match?"

"No. He said he wanted to wear something simple. We came up with the idea for a lumberjack costume. All he has to do is wear a flannel red plaid shirt, jeans, and work shoes. I bought him a rubber ax for a prop."

Carrie laughed. "What fun!"

I was about to ask Carrie what she planned to wear to her party, but the lieutenant was coming out of Pamela's office, so we paused.

"Was that Monique d'Albert I saw earlier?" he asked me. There wasn't even a snarl in his voice.

When I told him that he was right, he murmured, "hmm, interesting" and left the Roadrunner without another word.

Chapter 5

"Almost a perfect fit," Belle assured me as we gazed at my reflection in the floor-length mirror. We were in her guest room which doubled as her sewing room. Laddie and Mr. Big, Belle's little white dog, sat in the corner, their heads cocked to one side, watching us.

"I need to take in the bodice just a pinch here," she said, as she inserted a couple of pins into a seam. "And now for the cap."

Belle reached over to her sewing machine and plucked up something that looked a bit like an old-fashioned mob cap, except that it had a large red bow in the front that matched the red bow on my bathing suit. As she put it on me, she explained that the elastic in the cap should hold it on my head but that I could add a couple of bobby pins for extra security.

I grinned as I twirled around to get the full effect. Although the suit had short puff sleeves, allowing my arms to show, I was really covered up. The bodice of the navy blue suit looked something like a middy blouse that girls used to wear in gym class back in the day. The full skirt fell below my knees. My navy tights covered my legs, and I wore ballet slippers on my feet.

Practicality and utility didn't figure into the design of the outfit. Obviously, the Victorians didn't do much swimming in their bathing suits; they were beach costumes, if anything.

"What do you think?" I asked Belle.

"It's great fun," she replied, "and you look just like a Victorian woman at the beach. Are you planning to wear a mask?"

"No. The invitation said masks were optional. I suppose a few people might wear them, but everyone I've spoken to is going without."

"Well, you'll be all set as soon as I take in that seam. You're going to have to pose for some pictures before you and Brian go to the party."

"We will, I promise. He wasn't too wild about having to wear a costume, but when I came up with the lumberjack idea, he seemed to be comfortable with it. I haven't sprung the rubber ax on him yet, though."

"Oh, I'm sure he'll get into the spirit when you do."

"If he gets tired of carrying it around with him, he can just stash it in a corner somewhere."

Belle nodded. "Sounds like a plan. I bet you'll both have a great time!

"We'll be outside," she said. "Just leave your costume on the bed, and I'll fix that seam later. Come on, guys." Belle shooed the dogs out of the room ahead of her while I changed my clothes.

Then, I joined Belle on the patio while Laddie and Mr. Big ran around the backyard. It was pleasant to relax and chat as though my only care in the world was readying my costume for Carrie's Halloween party. I fully intended to allow myself to procrastinate until tomorrow when I really needed to get back to work.

After exhibiting my paintings at the prestigious Festival of the West Art Show over the weekend, I felt as though I were still recovering from a very busy two days. Granted, I'd worked at the gallery in the morning, but I hadn't so much as picked up a paintbrush in the two days since the show. I'd been so wiped out Monday that I'd spent the entire day resting until I'd attended the members' meeting at the Roadrunner. I knew Susan, who'd been the only other member of the Roadrunner to have a booth at the show, had felt as exhausted as I had.

Thankfully, for both Susan and me, the show had been worth every bit of effort we'd put into it. We'd been the only members of the Roadrunner to apply for the show. It was juried, which meant that not every artist who submitted an application was accepted. In fact, rumor had it that the jury members had approved only a handful of new-to-the-show artists. Because the Festival of the West drew art lovers from all over the United States and even a few from other countries, the crowds had been fantastic, and many buyers came prepared to spend money on art, unlike local shows, which typically featured a mix of art and crafts and drew a different crowd, many of whom viewed browsing as a form of recreation, something to do on the weekend.

At the show, I'd sold several large paintings, and Susan had sold two massive paper mâche animals—a wild mustang and a bison—in addition to several of her watercolors. Now we both needed to get to work to replenish our inventory. As one of the five artists Ian Adams was featuring in his Abstract Landscapes show at his gallery in Scottsdale in February, I was expected to produce new work for the exhibit, so I'd knew I'd have to maintain a regular painting schedule, starting tomorrow.

Until then, I planned to enjoy the rest of my downtime. The afternoon passed so quickly that I was surprised when the sky began to darken and it was time for Laddie and me to head home. Emma arrived a minute after we did, and Mona Lisa launched herself toward my daughter, who caught the excited cat in her arms.

"How was the exam?"

"Tough, but I think I did all right."

"I'm sure you did, Emma."

"Mrrr-ow!" Mona Lisa interrupted, demanding more attention.

"Did you miss me, Mona Lisa?"

My calico cat purred loudly enough that I heard her even though I was standing a few yards away.

"I'd say that's a safe bet. She was pretty much left to her own devices all afternoon, and I'm not going to be home tonight, either."

"Dinner with Susan, right?"

"Uh, huh."

"No problem. I'll be here."

"Would you like me to bring you some dinner from Miguel's?"

"No, thanks. I'll have some of that leftover casserole."

Sunday, after we'd broken down our booths, Susan and I had agreed that a celebratory dinner was in order. I realized that neither of us had mentioned it this morning when we were at the Roadrunner, so I texted her to make sure we were still on. When she replied that she was looking forward to it, I fed the pets and went to my bedroom to decide what to wear before getting ready to meet her.

After settling on a long green tunic top with black leggings, I took a quick shower, styled my hair, and swiped on some makeup. I draped one of my abstract dyed scarves around my shoulders and tied the ends in a square knot. I thought my watercolor design of blue, green, and orange hues brightened my ensemble.

After slipping on some black flats and turquoise earrings, I grabbed my purse, bade Emma and my pets good-bye, and went on my way. Despite having Emma for company, Laddie had looked up at me sadly with his big brown eyes when I departed, but since I knew he'd be just fine with Emma, I couldn't feel too guilty for leaving him behind. Of course, it was a matter of supreme indifference to Mona Lisa whether I stayed home with her or left the house, so she'd ignored me when I'd headed for the door.

Susan was pulling up across the street from Miguel's when I arrived. I parked and joined her at the door of the restaurant. We hadn't made a reservation since it typically wasn't crowded during the week, although the weekend was a different story entirely, and dinner reservations were definitely a must then.

We were seated right away at a small booth, and our server delivered a large bowl of corn chips along with salsa and guacamole. We passed on the margaritas, which were huge at Miguel's, and opted for iced tea instead. After Susan ordered enchiladas and I decided on fajitas, we toasted our success at the Festival of the West with iced tea and munched the corn chips while we waited for the server to bring our dinners.

"Did I tell you I got a commission to make a life-size desert tortoise from the Western Art Museum in Tucson?" Susan asked. "The director called me yesterday. I guess she stopped by my booth during the weekend sometime, but I don't remember her."

"That's great, Susan! I think it's fantastic that one of your sculptures will be displayed in a museum."

"I know. It's a first for me, and I'm kind of psyched about it. I think I'm going to deliver it myself, too. It's always fun to take a trip, and I'd like to see the museum. It's been there for about five years, but I haven't been down that way in a long time."

"Could I tag along? I'd like to see the museum, too, and the wind farm Brian manages isn't too far from there. Maybe he could meet us in Tucson."

"Sounds good to me. I'm thinking it'll probably be about a month before my tortoise is ready. I haven't started on him yet, but I'll at least do some sketching tomorrow. I already had a couple of other commissions lined up before this one, so I'll have to concentrate on them first."

"A little downtime was nice, but I really need to get back to work, too, or I won't be ready for the show at Ian's gallery."

Our server arrived with our food, then, and we enjoyed a leisurely dinner. It felt good to relax after our big weekend show. Following our meal, we ordered decaf, rather than dessert; after taking a few sips, I stifled a yawn and realized that I probably could have gone to sleep right there on the spot.

A sound like water rushing over rapids caught my attention, but when I looked around to see where it was coming from, I realized that I didn't need to look any farther than our booth. Susan reached into her purse and grabbed her cell phone. She must have changed her ringtone; I'd never heard that one before.

"Hi, Chip."

As soon as he started speaking, she switched to speaker mode so that I could hear their conversation.

"I think Monique's in trouble. She called me and said someone was trying to break into the gallery. I told her I'd come over, but it'll be at least fifteen minutes before I can get there. I just finished delivering six pizzas out on Mountain Crest Road. I already called the police."

"We'll go check it out, Chip," she told him as we rose, grabbed our bags, and headed for the door. We'd already paid the tab before lingering over coffee, so at least we weren't slowed down by having to signal our server and wait for the check. "See you in a few minutes."

"Let's take my car," I suggested. "We can come back later for yours."

"OK. I can't imagine why Monique wouldn't have called the police herself."

"I can't, either. That's a little odd."

Since Miguel's was only a few blocks away from the Roadrunner, it didn't take us long to get there. When we arrived, we saw the pulsating red lights of a couple of police cars in front of the gallery. Two uniformed cops were talking with a woman out front. At first, I thought it was Monique, but after I parked and took a closer look, I could tell it wasn't.

Susan and I jumped out of my SUV and walked over to the three.

"We're from the Roadrunner," Susan informed the officers. "We had a call about a break-in. What's going on?"

"As I was *trying* to explain to the officers if they would only *listen*, I was merely knocking on the door. Last I heard, that's not a crime."

"Looked more like you were pounding on the door to me," one of officers observed. "The gallery's closed, just like every other business on this street, so I think you'd better explain yourself."

I'd recognized the woman as soon as she began to talk. She was the gray-haired investigator who'd tried to speak to Monique after our members' meeting at the gallery.

"Nothing to explain, officer. I simply wanted to talk to the woman who's staying in the apartment upstairs."

"She already said she's not going to talk to you," I burst out and then instantly regretted it because I'd just confirmed that Monique was staying on the second floor. I didn't how the PI had found out, but I guessed she'd been following Monique. Perhaps she'd even overheard her talking to Chip at the Coffee Klatsch.

"That's right," Susan said. "Officers, this woman threatened Monique that she'd be watching her every move."

"Well, there's no sign of an attempted break-in, and it's not a crime to knock on the door," one of the cops said, "but I'd advise you to be careful, lady."

"Yeah," the other cop piped up. "You could find yourself on the wrong end of a harassment suit if you're stalking someone."

"I am *not* a stalker. I'm just doing my job," the PI pulled out her ID card and showed it to the officers.

"Do it someplace else. If you keep banging on this door, we'll have every right to bust you for disturbing the peace."

"I don't think so," the woman muttered, "but I'm leaving—for now." She walked the few yards to the end of the block and turned the corner. I figured she must have parked on the side street, rather than on Main Street.

"Is she gone?"

We all looked up and saw Monique peering out of a second-floor window.

"Looks that way," Susan told her. "Are you all right?"

"I . . . I got scared. I thought someone was breaking into the gallery."

"Looks like everything's under control, Jake," one of the officers said to the other. "We'd better get back on patrol."

"Thank you for coming," I said.

"Yes, ma'am," Officer Jake said. "Just doing our job."

Red lights now off, the police cruisers left, and Chip pulled into the spot directly in front of the gallery where one of the police cars had been parked.

"Chip!" Monique called from the upstairs window. "That awful woman was trying to get to me!"

"Who do you mean?" Chip asked.

"It was that old private investigator who came into the gallery looking for Monique after our members' meeting last night," I said, "and she was pounding on the door. She claimed she wasn't breaking in, and there aren't any signs of forced entry, so the cops didn't arrest her, but they told her to knock it off, or they'd charge her with disturbing the peace."

"Oh, Chip," Monique moaned. "I'm *so* scared. Can you stay with me? I'm afraid she'll come back, and I'm all alone here."

"Uh, sure, but I have deliveries until eleven tonight. You can drive around with me till then if you don't want to stay here."

Susan glared at her nephew. "Don't be ridiculous. I'll stay with her tonight. You'd better get back to work before your father realizes you're AWOL."

"I guess so," Chip agreed reluctantly. "I'll check with you later."

After Chip left, Susan dug the key to the gallery out of her purse and told Monique we'd be coming in. I could tell she was more than a little bit put out about the situation, and I also had the feeling she didn't want Chip to become more involved with Monique.

As soon as we stepped inside, Susan turned on all the lights in the gallery and locked the door. We headed upstairs to find the door to the apartment closed. Susan rapped sharply on the door.

"Monique, open the door!"

"Who is it?"

"Susan and Amanda."

"Is anybody else with you?"

"No," Susan said impatiently. "Open up."

We could hear the rattle of the safety chain before Monique inched the door backwards a couple of inches and cautiously peeked out before stepping out of the way to let us in. Up to this point, I'd thought Monique's reaction had been overly dramatic, but when I saw her, I realized that she wasn't just playacting. She was so unnerved that she was shaking.

"Everything's all right now," I told Monique. "That woman left. The police told her they'd arrest her for disturbing the peace if she kept banging on the door."

"I know. I heard them, but I don't think she'll stop. I'm sure she's been following me."

"Maybe you should talk to her and get it over with," Susan suggested.

"No way. Nicole's out to get me any way she can. I know she hired that PI."

"Who's Nicole?" I asked.

"My husband's daughter, my darling step-daughter," she replied bitterly. "The woman hates me!"

As soon as Monique spoke, I remembered Nicole's name from the news report I'd heard about the dispute over Edward McCall's will.

"She thinks I killed her father!" Monique continued. "It's so ridiculous. I wasn't even at home when Ed died, and he was *not* murdered. His own doctor signed his death certificate."

"Maybe she thinks if she casts suspicious on you, the judge would look more favorably on her case," Susan said.

"You know about our fight over Ed's will?" Monique asked in surprise.

"There was a story about it on the national news this morning," I said.

"Already? I guess it was inevitable. My lawyer warned me that it would be all over the news. That's one of the reasons I decided to come back to Lonesome Valley. I was hoping a bunch of reporters wouldn't track me down here. Now that investigator's found me, and she might tip them off."

"She's gone for now, anyway. We won't have any problem keeping her out of the gallery, either. Why don't you try to get some sleep? I'll stay in the guest room; I can call Chip and tell him he doesn't need to come over after he gets off work."

"No, please. I want him to come. I want a *man* here to protect me."

I could tell that Susan thought Monique's request was beyond ridiculous, but she was so upset that Susan gave in.

"Well, all right. He can sleep on the sofa here in the living room. There's only one way in here, and nobody will be able to get past him," Susan assured her. "Now why don't you go to bed, lock your door and your window, and try to get some sleep. I'll be right across the hall in the guest room if you need anything."

Monique nodded and did as Susan suggested. We could hear the dead bolt on her bedroom door slide closed.

"What do you make of that?" Susan whispered. "Is she really scared?"

"Sure seems like it to me."

"Yeah, I thought so, too. I think there's more to the story than she told us."

"So do I."

"Amanda, you might as well go on home. I think two babysitters for Monique are already two too many."

With promises to call each other in the morning, we said good-bye, and Susan went downstairs to lock up again after I left.

As I pulled away from the curb, I thought I saw a movement across the street. I drove on, circled the block, and came back to check it out.

Sure enough, I had seen something.

Smoking a cigarette, the gray-haired private investigator was standing in an alcove between two of the stores across from the Roadrunner, and she was staring up at Monique's bedroom window.

Chapter 6

As I slowed my car, wondering whether I should jump out and tell the woman to move along, a police cruiser rounded the corner and pulled over to the curb. In my rearview mirror, I spotted one of the officers who'd answered the call to the gallery get out of his car and motion to the woman.

Figuring that the police were keeping an eye on the Roadrunner, I drove home after pulling over to text Susan to let her know that the investigator was still hanging around.

The following day, I jumped out of bed, knowing that it was time for me to get back to work. That's exactly what I did after a quick trip to the park with Laddie and a light breakfast of toast and tea. At mid-morning, I paused, stepped back from my newest expressionistic abstract landscape, and took a long look at it. Viewing the painting from farther away gave me a different perspective. Although I liked my color palette with its subtle hues, I could see that the composition needed a slight correction. Luckily, it would be an easy fix, but it would have to wait until this afternoon because I had an errand to run that couldn't wait.

I quickly traded my paint-spattered t-shirt and jeans for a tunic top and skirt and then draped one of my abstract silk scarves around my neck. I grabbed my purse and the small canvas I'd painted depicting my aunt's beloved longtime companion, her tabby cat Max.

Aunt Laura's birthday was coming up next week, and I never should have waited so long to have the painting framed, but I'd been so involved with preparations for my display at the Festival of the West that I'd neglected to take care of it. I was hoping that Brooks might do me a favor and expedite the framing since he not only managed the Lonesome Valley Resort but also owned the art gallery and frame shop in the Resort's mall.

"Mommy will be back soon," I assured my anxious pet on my way out the door, but, as usual, he looked at me dolefully with his big, brown eyes as if to say "how could you leave me?"

I hoped that Brooks would be available when I dropped the painting off because he was far more likely to put a rush on my order than his employees would be.

When I arrived at the Resort, I decided to park in the lot, rather than go to the valet drop-off area. It was a glorious October day, the sun bright in a cloudless sky, and I felt like walking. Brooks's art gallery and frame shop were about halfway down the wide mall, and as I passed boutiques, gift shops, and jewelry stores on the way, I glanced into their windows, but I didn't stop to browse.

Since I knew my aunt favored dark wood frames, I had already chosen which frame I wanted to order. As I stepped into the frame shop, I could see that I was in luck. Brooks himself was at the front counter, talking with a customer. All I had to do was bide my time until he was free. I wandered over to a display on the side wall and idly looked it over before glancing back at Brooks, who hadn't noticed me, and realizing that his customer was none other than Monique.

Remembering that Pamela had said that Monique used to date Brooks, I knew that the two already had a connection. Curious as to what Monique was up to, I moved a bit closer and perked up my ears.

"Brooksie, please," she whined softly.

"Sorry, Monique, I can't do it." Brooks sounded regretful. "I wish I could fit in a show for you in my art gallery, but I have signed contracts with artists for exhibitions for the next two years. Legally, I can't change those; I have to fulfill my end of the bargain. I really am sorry. You know I'd do it for you if I could."

Monique sighed. I heard what sounded like a little hiccup.

"Don't cry, Monique," Brooks urged. "Don't you know I'd do anything for you if only I could?"

"I guess," she sniffed, dabbing her eyes with a tissue he'd handed her.

"Now, here's something I *can* do. You'll be my guest here at the Resort. There's no need for you to stay in that apartment above the Roadrunner; it's not safe."

I figured that Monique had already told Brooks about the private investigator who was following her.

"I'd like to, Brooks, but I'm afraid I can't afford a suite here, even though Ed left me everything in his will. His estate is all tied up because of that mean daughter of his. She'd do anything to make sure I don't inherit. I barely have enough funds to get by on."

"Don't worry about that. When I said you'll be my guest, I meant it. I'm comping you the suite; there'll be no charge."

"Oh, Brooks, *really*?" I could picture Monique batting her eyelashes just then.

"Really! You know you can count on me."

"Well, aren't you the sweetest man," she murmured, leaning across the counter and giving him a kiss.

Monique certainly had met with success when she worked her wiles on Brooks, but I thought it was most likely for the best that she wouldn't be staying in the apartment above the Roadrunner, especially after last night's incident. I was sure Susan would think the same, but I wasn't too certain about Chip.

While Brooks picked up the phone and directed his staff to prepare a suite for Monique, I moved to the counter, hoping to catch his attention, but he had eyes only for Monique, and he didn't even notice me standing there, although I was only a few feet away from him.

After he hung up the phone, I decided to take the direct approach.

"Hi, Monique. Brooks, I was hoping to catch you. I have a painting that I need to have framed."

"No problem, Amanda. Lew can help you. We're just on our way out."

"Isn't Brooks just the *best*, Amanda?" Monique gushed. "He's invited me to stay here, where nobody will bother me."

"Yes, very generous," I agreed.

"Lew!" Brooks called to his employee.

"Uh, Brooks, could you please do me a favor and put a rush on my frame job? I wouldn't ordinarily ask, but the painting's a gift for my aunt whose birthday is next week. She lives in Kansas City, so I'll have to ship it."

"Of course, Amanda," he said as Lew emerged from the back room. "Lew, take care of it please."

"Sure thing."

"May I see your painting?" Monique asked.

After I placed it on the counter, Monique exclaimed, "How adorable! I just love cats, don't you?"

I nodded. "I have a calico cat myself. Her name is Mona Lisa."

"Oh, I love that. It's the *cutest* name for an artist's cat."

"Monique," Brooks interrupted. "Let me show you to your suite. We'd better get going. I have a meeting in ten minutes."

"'Bye, bye, Amanda," Monique said, as she took the arm Brooks offered and clung to her former boyfriend. "See you at the Roadrunner."

"I won't be there for the rest of the week, but I'll see you at the party."

"Party? What party?" Brooks asked.

Chapter 7

The couple were out of earshot before Monique replied. I turned my attention to Lew, who wrote up my order for me, promising to complete the frame job by Friday and arrange to ship my painting to my aunt. Pleased that I'd taken care of her gift, I left the Resort and walked through the parking lot to my SUV. Just as I sat down behind the wheel, my cell phone rang. I glanced at the display and saw that the call was coming from the Roadrunner. Since the number was the gallery's landline, it could have been any member calling, but it turned out to be Pamela.

"Hi, Amanda. I hear there was some excitement here at the gallery last night," she said.

"Susan must have filled you in."

"Yes, she called me this morning and told me all about the investigator showing up and scaring Monique. I hope it doesn't happen again."

"You can rest assured it won't, at least not at night, anyway, because Monique has moved to the Resort. I was just there to drop off a painting at Brooks's frame shop, and I heard him offer to comp her a suite. Monique was more than happy to accept. She definitely seemed relieved; I think she was scared out of her wits last night."

"Really? Well, under the circumstances, I think it's for the best."

"So do I. Downtown's pretty much deserted after closing, and the police can't keep an eye on the Roadrunner all the time, although I know they came back by last night and found that the PI had returned. I guess she's been following Monique, and Monique's on edge about it. She should be safe at the Resort, though. Brooks has plenty of security there."

"Maybe we better schedule a few more people to work when Monique's turn to staff the gallery comes up."

"It probably wouldn't hurt."

Pamela sighed. "I wish. . . oh, never mind. It's just that it seems as though whenever Monique's around, trouble follows. Oh, well, not much I can do about it except increase the staffing. She's not scheduled to work until next week, so that gives me a few days to find some volunteers to work extra hours."

"I can give you a half day next week, if you can't find anyone else."

"Thanks, Amanda. I may have to take you up on that, but I hate to do it. I know how busy you're going to be getting ready for your show at the Ian Adams Gallery. I'll let you know either way."

I didn't hear from Pamela again until Saturday morning, and then she told me she'd found enough people to help so that I wouldn't have to interrupt my painting to go to the Roadrunner the following week. I'd maintained a consistent work schedule in the meantime, and I fully intended to keep it up, but I planned on allowing myself some downtime on the weekends, starting that very evening when Brian and I would be attending Carrie's party.

My Victorian costume was hanging on the back of my closet door, and I'd laid out the little mob cap with the cute bow, my tights, and the box containing my ballet slippers on top of my dresser so that I wouldn't have to scurry around to put my costume together when it was time to get ready. As soon as I began puttering around in the bedroom, readying my outfit, Laddie sensed that something was up.

I knew he'd be happy to hang out with his little buddy Mr. Big, but he didn't realize that he'd be spending the evening next door yet, and he stuck to me like glue until I took him out to the backyard for a game of fetch.

Normally, Brian would have been back home in Lonesome Valley by this time, but he still wasn't back in town. He'd had an unexpected visit from a corporate bigwig on Friday, and the man wasn't scheduled to return to Texas until early afternoon. Brian planned to leave as soon as he dropped the guy off at the airport in Tucson. As long as all went as scheduled, he'd arrive in plenty of time for us to go to the Halloween party.

I giggled to myself when I thought about being a guest at a costume party. It had literally been decades since I'd dressed up for Halloween. Of course, the holiday was still ten days away, but Carrie hadn't wanted to schedule her party the Saturday before Halloween because the Roadrunner was hosting the pumpkin painting event that day.

When Brian called from Phoenix after stopping to buy gas, I figured he'd make it in time for the party. I wrapped up my painting for the day and popped my oil paints into my tiny freezer for storage until I was ready to use them again. After taking a shower, I lounged around in my robe until Brian phoned to let me know he'd be over in ten minutes. I quickly donned my costume, securing my ruffled cap with a couple of bobby pins.

After I heard his tap on the front door and my daughter greeting him, I emerged from my bedroom and came into the living room.

"Cute costume!" he exclaimed, hugging me. "It's a Victorian swim suit, right?"

"Right, although I doubt that the Victorians who wore this sort of get-up did much swimming. I thought you'd recognize it, history buff that you are."

"I really like it. It's unique."

"Glad you approve, kind sir," I said, clutching my skirt and dipping into a curtsy.

"Oh, I most definitely do approve. Of course, you'd look great in anything!"

"You're looking mighty handsome yourself."

"Mom, don't forget Brian's present," Emma prompted me.

"Ah, here we are." I handed him a long white box wrapped with a bright red ribbon.

Brian looked at me quizzically. "What's this? It looks like a box from the florist."

"Don't worry. I didn't get you flowers. Open it!"

Brian proceeded to rip off the ribbon and remove the lid from the box. As soon as he saw the rubber ax, he grinned. He laid the box on the coffee table and took out the prop, running his thumb along its fake blade.

"Rubber, huh? It looks real enough."

"I thought it would make a good addition to your costume."

Brian slung the ax over his shoulder and struck a pose. "Do I look like Paul Bunyan?"

I laughed, and Emma took out her phone and asked us to pose for a couple of pictures. Of course, Laddie, who'd been buzzing around the entire time, had to take part. At least he cooperated when I told him to sit, and he looked straight at Emma with his big brown eyes when she said "cheese."

"Have fun!" Emma said as we departed with Laddie in tow.

"You, too! See you later." Emma and Matt were going to a party, too, although it wasn't a costume party, but a gathering of several of their friends.

Belle insisted on taking some pictures of us in our costumes, too, while Dennis wrangled the canines.

"We'd better be on our way," Brian said. "It's almost seven now."

I stooped to pet Laddie, and Mr. Big crowded in for some attention, too.

They followed us to the door, but Dennis distracted them so that we could slip out.

When we arrived at Carrie's house, we found only a few cars parked out front. Brian pulled up in back of one of them.

"I wonder where everybody is," I said as Brian opened the car door for me. "I thought most of the members of the gallery were going to be here, and I know Carrie invited quite a few others."

"We're right on the dot," Brian told me, consulting his watch. He was one of the few men I knew who still customarily wore one. He gazed up at Carrie's three-story Victorian residence, complete with a cupola surrounded by a balcony. "This is some house, probably built in the 1890s I'd guess."

"You'd be right. Carrie's great-great grandfather made a fortune in mining and built it. It's been in the family ever since. Carrie lives here with her grandmother."

"Plenty of room for two people; that's for sure."

"Yes, it's huge. I've been in it once before, when I visited Carrie's studio. She converted one of the second-floor bedrooms into her studio, and that's where she makes her jewelry."

As we approached the house, floodlights came on, illuminating the front yard and porch. Two huge jack-o-lanterns sat on pedestals beside the front door, but, otherwise, the nicely landscaped property was devoid of Halloween decorations.

The front door swung open, and an out-of-breath Carrie invited us inside.

"Carrie, are you all right?" I asked.

"Yes. A breaker switch flipped off, and I was having trouble getting to it. We had the house re-wired a few months ago, and I almost panicked when I couldn't get the box open. I had to put a code in, and I couldn't remember it. Finally, Gram found it. Anyway, problem solved. I love your costumes, by the way."

"Thanks, yours, too. You look fantastic! Your gown is such a beautiful hue of green, just perfect with your hair."

Carrie was dressed quite regally in a long emerald satin gown. She wore a sparkling rhinestone necklace, a huge twinkling brooch, and a diamante tiara in her hair.

"Thanks. It's such fun to dress in costume."

"Are we the first to arrive?"

"Not quite. Dawn and Dave are here. I guess everybody else is planning on being fashionably late."

Brian had been gazing admiringly around the large living room while Carrie and I chatted.

"They don't make 'em like this any more," he commented. "Just look at the grain in this wood." His hand brushed the trim around the door, and he glanced at the wide walnut baseboards. "Plaster walls, too. Wow!"

"Yes, we've preserved the woodwork and the plaster walls, although the kitchen and bathrooms have been remodeled a few times since the house was built. Oh, and all the old glass chandeliers and stained-glass windows around the house are original, too." Carrie turned and pointed out some of the beautiful old stained glass.

"Amazing," Brian said.

"Glad you like it. How about a snack? The caterers have set up a nice buffet in the dining room. Apple cider's in the punch bowl, and beer's in the kitchen."

Carrie led us into the dining room, where Dawn and Dave were sampling pigs-in-a-blanket.

"I see you didn't have to go far to find your costume, Dave," I said.

"Right to my closet," he chuckled.

He wore his police dress blues, and Dawn was attired in a long white apron over her white shirt and black pants. She'd topped off her outfit with a white baker's hat. A wooden spoon and a rubber spatula peeked out of a deep pocket in her apron and a recipe card was stashed into a smaller pocket.

As Dawn and I were admiring each other's costumes, the doorbell rang, and a crowd of party guests appeared. Soon, the event was in full swing. By the time Brian and I had helped ourselves to some snacks and a cup of cider from the huge punch bowl, the dining room overflowed with partygoers. We drifted into the large den next to the kitchen to find some space.

"I'll take our plates and cups to the kitchen," Brian volunteered. "Would you like a beer?"

"No, thanks. I'm good for now."

"I think I'll grab one. Be right back." He flashed a grin as I handed him my plate and cup.

Brian barely missed colliding with Chip as he came into the den, but although the plates he was carrying tipped precariously, he managed to keep them balanced.

"Sorry, Brian," Chip said. "Or should I say Mr. Bunyon?"

He laughed. "No harm done, and Brian will do just fine, *Dr. Baxter.*"

In a white lab coat with a stethoscope hanging from around his neck, its end tucked into his coat pocket, Chip did indeed look like an M.D.

"Nice touch, Chip," I said, pointing to a plastic name tag pinned to his pocket that read 'Dr. Travis Baxter.'"

"Thanks. I had it made at the copy shop. Do I look like a real doc?"

"You could have fooled me."

"And look at you. That's some costume! You're a real bathing beauty," he said with an exaggerated wink. "Say, you haven't seen Monique, have you? She was supposed to meet me here."

"No, not yet."

"I wanted to pick her up, but she said her dressmaker had to make an adjustment for her costume, and she was going to change there, so she asked me to meet her here."

"I'm sure she'll be along any minute."

Just then Brian came back into the den. "There's a big commotion out front. Some guy dressed in a chauffeur's uniform came up to the door and said that everyone should come outside. Shall we see what all the fuss is about?"

Chip and I joined Brian, and we walked back through the house to the front door. Most of the guests had already gathered on the wide front porch. When we joined them, we saw a black limousine parked at the end of Carrie's front sidewalk. We didn't know whether the chauffeur was a costumed guest or a real chauffeur, but whoever he was, he opened the trunk and pulled out a narrow red rug, which he proceeded to unroll onto the sidewalk. Although the "red carpet" was only about twelve feet long, we got the idea.

A celebrity was about to make an appearance.

Chapter 8

The chauffeur returned to the limo and opened the back door. He extended his hand to the occupant, helped her out of the vehicle, and quickly stepped aside.

Blowing kisses, Monique, dressed in a long strapless candy pink silk gown and matching above-elbow gloves, sashayed down the red carpet, her dangling shoulder-dusting earrings and glitzy necklace twinkling in the lights along the sidewalk. As she moved, the huge bow on the back of the dress dipped and swayed. She wore bright red lipstick and her blond hair framed her face with soft waves. Her waist was cinched with a pink silk belt, and wide glittering bracelets worn over her gloves adorned both wrists.

"It's Marilyn Monroe!" Dave shouted, and the crowd began to clap.

"She'd certainly take the prize for best costume, if there was a prize," Carrie commented.

"It's the dress Marilyn wore in *Gentlemen Prefer Blondes*, Brian whispered to me. Not only was he a history buff, but he was also a fan of old movies, and he remembered the details of classic films much better than I did.

"Oh, right. I thought I'd seen it somewhere. Monique certainly looks the part."

As she approached the porch, Chip rushed to her, offering his arm. She clung to him as they came up the steps onto the porch where she was immediately surrounded by a group of costumed admirers. As Brian and I stood back from the crush, I thought about how funny the scene looked with the glamorous Monique surrounded by men in all kinds of costumes, including a biker, a wolf, a super hero, and Dracula, among others.

While all the hubbub was going on, I looked around to see if any of the neighbors were watching the spectacle, and I noticed a thin woman with wispy gray hair observing the scene from the porch of the home across the street. She wasn't trying to hide her interest, as some people might have done under the same circumstances. In fact, she was waving.

Carrie, who was standing beside us, waved back and beckoned the woman to come over, but she just smiled and shook her head.

"That's Gram's friend Patricia. We invited her to the party, but she doesn't like crowds, so Gram told her to be sure to watch our house so she could see all the costumes."

As Monique began inching toward the front door, the group slowly followed, crowding into the living room. Carrie began urging the guests to help themselves to the goodies set out in the dining room, and eventually most of the partygoers dispersed enough so that we finally felt we had room to breathe.

Monique was still surrounded by several guests, and I could see that Chip wasn't going to be able to monopolize his date. When Susan arrived a few minutes later, dressed like Amelia Earhart, ready to pilot a plane, Chip left Monique's side and greeted his aunt with a kiss on the cheek.

"Looks like your date's the center of attention," Susan said to her nephew.

"I know," Chip said with a sigh. "I guess I'll go get something to eat."

"He doesn't exactly seem devastated," Brian observed, as Chip headed for the dining room.

"That's my nephew for you. There's not much that he takes too seriously, including his flirtations," Susan said.

We retreated to the library, a huge room lined with custom shelves filled with books, many of them older leather-bound volumes. I knew that Brian would have to have a good look at the books, and he soon excused himself and began browsing through them while Susan and I chatted. It wasn't too long before Valerie and Frank, both dressed as artists wearing voluminous white paint-spattered smocks and perky red berets on their heads, showed up. Several paint brushes were tucked in Valerie's pocket while tubes of paint peeked out of the pocket in Frank's smock.

Since the couple was holding hands when they came into the library, I assumed that they'd gotten over their spat. I hoped that Frank would have enough sense not to ignore his wife in favor of Monique, but it turned out that they'd arrived after Monique's big entrance, and they weren't yet aware that she was at the party.

When Frank offered to bring us all drinks, Brian and I passed, but Susan and Valerie took him up on it, and he departed, promising to be back in a flash. When he still hadn't returned after fifteen minutes, Valerie left to find him.

"Uh, oh. I have a feeling this might not end well," I said.

"Maybe we should go distract Valerie. I'd hate for them to have more troubles over Monique. They've only been married a few months. They should still be in the honeymoon phase."

"OK. We can try," I said although I had my doubts that we'd be able to head off Valerie if she found Frank hanging around Monique. "We'll be back in a bit," I told Brian.

He nodded and whispered, "You should see all the first editions. This place is better than a library. These books are worth a fortune! I hope Carrie and her grandmother know what they have here."

"We do indeed, Mr.?"

I hadn't seen Carrie's grandmother come in, but all of a sudden she was at Brian's elbow.

"Hudson, Brian Hudson—and please do call me Brian. You must be Carrie's grandmother."

"Yes, Betty Shaw's my name."

Dressed in a vintage white nurse's uniform complete with a white cap perched on her head, white stockings and shoes, and a blue cape, Betty cut quite the figure.

While she and Brian shook hands, we all complimented each other on our costumes, and Betty told us that her mother had been a nurse back in the fifties, and that she had worn that very uniform to work.

Our mission had been delayed for a few minutes, and by the time Susan and I left the library in search of Valerie, Betty had unlocked the only free-standing bookcase in the room and was showing Brian some signed, special editions. Although he acknowledged our departure with a little wave, it was obvious that he'd be tied up for a while.

We searched all the rooms on the first floor without finding either Frank or Valerie. We didn't spot Monique, either. By now, the place was quite crowded, and Carrie had turned on some music. In the den, the last room we looked in, some of the guests were dancing, but the music was so loud that Susan and I couldn't hear each other. I motioned her to follow me into the kitchen where we could talk. Luckily, it was such a large area that we had no trouble staying out of the way of the caterers who bustled back and forth, carrying trays of food into the dining room and replenishing the bottles of beer set out on the counter.

"We don't seem to be having any luck. Shall we try upstairs?" I suggested.

"I guess so. I don't know where else they could be unless they went outside."

We were about to go back to the wide staircase with its highly polished banister that led from the entryway to the second floor, when one of the caterers, who had overheard us, pointed out that there was a back stairway next to the pantry. We thanked her and proceeded up the narrow stairs, which were enclosed on both sides.

"These stairs must have been the ones the servants used back in the old days," Susan guessed as we climbed.

When we reached the second floor-landing, we could see that the stairs went on up to the third floor, although there was a rope across them. We had to open a door to access the second story. We emerged in an alcove, noticing that the door itself was rather discreetly hidden, whether by design or accident. I speculated that the builder of the huge home had intended it to be unobtrusive, but I really didn't know for sure.

With rooms on both sides, a wide hallway ran the length of the second floor. We didn't see anybody, and all the doors were closed, except at the end of the hallway, where the lights were on in Carrie's studio. As we walked toward the studio, Count Dracula bounded up the stairs and went into the restroom, which was posted with a large sign so that the partygoers couldn't miss it.

We entered the studio and saw several of our members, Monique included, crowded around Carrie, who was showing them some of her jewelry creations.

"Have any of you seen Valerie or Frank?" I asked.

Carrie shook her head. Monique had a cat-who-just-swallowed-the-canary look on her face.

"Monique?" I asked.

"Uh, I think maybe they went outside."

"I had some heat lamps set up out on the patio, so it wouldn't be too cold to hang out there," Carrie told us.

"What a great idea!" Susan exclaimed.

We went back to the first floor, this time by the much-easier-to-navigate front stairs.

"I guess there's not much point looking for Valerie and Frank now. Sounds as though it's too late," I said. "Did you see the look on Monique's face? There was something she wasn't telling us."

"It's easy enough to guess. I bet Valerie found Frank fawning over Monique and had a meltdown."

"I think so, too. Well, we'd better get back to the library. If I don't miss my guess, Brian's still examining those old books, and he's lost all track of time.

At the bottom of the stairs, we ran into Brooks, dressed in a Dracula costume.

"I thought you were upstairs," Susan said in confusion.

"Me? No, I just arrived. I got delayed with a minor problem at the Resort. You haven't seen Monique by any chance, have you?"

"She's upstairs in Carrie's studio right now," I told him. "Last room on the right."

As Brooks took the stairs two at a time, the other man dressed in a Dracula costume descended. Brooks stopped and laughed. It looked as though he were about to say something to the other man, but he continued down the steps as though Brooks weren't even there. He brushed past us, barely avoiding running into Susan. Although the black half-mask he wore over his eyes partially obscured his face, the spicy scent of his aftershave lingered.

"Rude," Susan said as he stalked off, but he was out of earshot by then. "I wonder who he is."

I shrugged. "No idea, but he couldn't be one of our members. Nobody at the Roadrunner is that tall—or that obnoxious."

"Well, I guess no harm's been done, but I'm curious. I might check with Carrie later, if I get a chance."

As I'd surmised, Brian was still absorbed in the extensive book collection that he'd discovered in the library.

"Miss me?" I teased, knowing full well that he'd probably forgotten I'd even left the room for a while.

"Naturally," he said quickly with an impish grin. He returned the volume he'd been perusing to its glass-fronted case, turned the key, and pocketed it. "I need to return the key to Betty before I forget. She said she'd be in the kitchen."

"I think I'll stay here for a while," Susan said, sinking into a plush distressed leather chair. "I've been on my feet all day, and I'm getting a bit tired."

"OK; we'll catch up with you later."

As Brian and I made our way through the crowd, which seemed to have grown since my last foray with Susan, I spotted a short woman in a Little Red Riding Hood costume carrying a basket. Although I didn't recognize her, I stopped to tell her how much I liked her costume. Only then did I see that she wore a mask in the guise of a small girl. However, when she thanked me, it was obvious that she was much older than her character, and I suspected Little Red Riding Hood might be Dorothy, Dawn's mother, although she sounded a bit hoarse.

She was off before I could ask her, though, and I too distracted by the sight of Ralph costumed as the cowardly lion from *The Wizard of Oz* to try to catch up with her. Ralph was easy to recognize, even though he'd drawn some whiskers on his face, and a halo of yarn served as his mane.

"Ralph, what a great costume!"

"Thanks, Amanda, I didn't intend to come at first, but then I remembered that my neighbor wore this outfit his wife made him for Halloween a few years ago, and he offered to lend it to me, so I thought, why not? Betty told me she's going to have the caterers set up a dessert table out on the patio, so I'm headed that way."

"Dessert sounds good. Maybe we'll join you in a few minutes. We have a little errand to take care of first."

"OK. By the way, your costumes are great, too! That ax is a nice touch, Brian. See you later."

I was a little surprised that Brian hadn't parked the rubber ax in a corner somewhere by now, but he was still cheerfully toting it with him wherever we went.

We didn't find Betty in the kitchen, so we wandered into the dining room to look for her, but she wasn't there, either.

"Maybe she's outside," I speculated. "She might be helping the caterers set up the dessert table."

"All right. Let's check out there," Brian said, as he took my hand and we threaded our way through the throng.

As soon as Brian slid open the patio door, we spotted Betty standing near the dessert table, talking to Chip. I had to smile at the sight of the two "medical professionals" in what looked like a serious consultation. Munching on a brownie, Ralph was sitting in a little group gathered around the fire pit. With the heat lamps on and the fire pit glowing, we weren't cold at all, although the temperature had dropped considerably since our arrival.

As Brian handed Betty the bookcase key, he thanked her for allowing him to browse through her precious signed first editions, and she invited him to come over for another look any time.

"I just may take you up on that," he told her.

"Please do. Not too many people are interested in old books."

"Well, I'm fascinated, and you certainly have some rare ones. It's a pleasure to be able to see them all in one spot."

While Brian and Betty were talking, I happened to glance up at the old mansion. The cupola that Brian had commented on was on the side of the house, overlooking the driveway, which led to what had originally been a carriage house in the eighteen hundreds but had been converted into a garage decades earlier, when automobiles became more popular than horses and carriages for transportation.

As I was about to look away, a movement caught my eye. The door leading onto the cupola's balcony swung open, and I saw Monique in the doorway.

"What in the world?" I pointed upwards as Brian and Betty looked at me.

"She shouldn't be up there," Betty said. "I know I locked the door to that room because it could be dangerous out on that balcony. We're planning to have it replaced."

"Do you think I should call to her to go back inside?" Brian asked.

"Better not. I'm afraid she might get startled. I'll go find Carrie, so she can go up there and tell Monique to come back in."

"Last I saw her, Carrie was upstairs in the studio," I told Betty as she hurried off.

Monique had wandered around to the front of the cupola's balcony, so we couldn't see her anymore. As we continued to watch, I gripped Brian's arm, anxious for Carrie to coax Monique back inside.

Then we heard a shriek.

"No!" Monique screamed, and suddenly we saw her appear, pitching backwards and hitting the low railing of the balcony. There was a sickening splintering sound as the wood gave way, and Monique fell to the concrete driveway below.

Chapter 9

"Someone call 9-1-1," I yelled as Chip, Brian, and I raced to Monique. Brian and I had both left our phones in his car, but I knew many of the guests probably had brought theirs along to the party.

Monique lay totally still. Chip knelt beside her and felt for a pulse.

"She's alive!" he proclaimed.

Monique must have heard him because she opened her eyes just then. She moaned and whispered something to Chip, but I couldn't hear what she said. She'd spoken so softly that Chip couldn't hear her, either, so he leaned in closer as she continued to mumble. By now, all the guests who had been on the patio had gathered around.

"An ambulance is on the way," Ralph called, as he limped toward us. "The dispatcher said not to move her."

"I hear the sirens already," Dawn said. "Hold on, Monique. Help's on the way."

Holding Monique's hand, Chip squeezed it in an effort to reassure her.

"I'm going out to the street and flag down that ambulance," Brian told me before he rushed to the end of the driveway.

Monique opened her eyes again and looked at Chip.

"Air, air!" she said, and this time she spoke just loudly enough that I could hear her.

"Stand back, everyone!" Chip cried. "She's having trouble breathing! Back up!"

As we began to move away, the ambulance screeched to a stop at the end of the driveway, and Brian pointed the way for the attendants, who didn't waste any time assessing the situation and transferring Monique onto a backboard. Before we knew it, with red lights flashing and siren wailing, they were on their way to Lonesome Valley Hospital, only a few miles distant.

Staring at the pool of blood on the driveway, I shivered both because of the horror of Monique's fall and the realization that my short little puff sleeves were no barrier to the cool night air. Brian put his arm around me and pulled me close.

"I didn't see it happen, but do you suppose Monique tripped and fell against the railing?" Dawn asked.

"No, I don't think it was an accident." I told her. "To me, it looked as though she was pushed. What do you think, Brian?"

"Yes, I'm sure of it, but we couldn't see anybody else up there with her from where we were standing."

"We'd better find Dave and let him know."

"Right here," Dave said as he came up behind his wife. Both Brian and I told him what we'd seen, and he immediately herded all the guests and caterers who'd come outside when they'd heard the ambulance's siren back into the house.

Passing the word that nobody should leave before they'd spoken to the police, Dave took charge. While the partygoers were trooping back inside, he called the station and I figured that Lieutenant Belmont was bound to show up soon.

In tears, Carrie and Betty were standing in the kitchen. When Carrie saw me, she dabbed her eyes with a tissue and asked if I'd seen what had happened. I hated to tell her, but I explained briefly what Brian and I had observed.

Betty put her hand over her mouth and gasped. "The door to the cupola was locked. I locked it myself, and I double-checked, before the party started, to make sure that all the rooms on the third floor were locked. I even tied a rope across both stairways to keep the guests from going up there."

"Where do you keep the key?" I asked.

"Around the corner there, by the back stairway." We followed Betty, and she pointed out a pegboard that held several keys, all neatly labeled. It was obvious that anybody could have taken the key to the cupola at any time. That fact wasn't lost on Carrie or Betty.

"Oh, no!" Carrie groaned. "The key's gone. Monique must have unlocked the door herself. I hope she's going to be all right."

Although I thought that Monique had been very seriously injured, I certainly didn't have the experience to judge her condition. She'd been alive when she was whisked off to the hospital, so there was hope.

"Let's go into the other room, so you can sit down," Brian suggested.

Carrie nodded and she and her grandmother accompanied us as we made our way to the library. When we passed through the entryway, Dave was directing traffic, not allowing anybody to leave or go to the second floor.

The library turned out to be a good choice since it was the least crowded room downstairs. We all found seats clustered around Susan, who was still sitting in the same chair where we'd left her earlier. There were a few clusters of guests scattered around the large room, but I noticed that Brooks, standing next to one of the bookshelves, was all by himself. He was pretending to study the volumes, probably because he didn't want to talk to anyone. Since he had once been engaged to Monique, I believed he was quite upset.

"I just heard what happened," Susan informed us. "I can't believe it, but it was so warm and cozy in here that I actually dozed off for a while. I must have been more tired than I realized. I was so out of it, I didn't hear the ambulance."

Tears dribbled down Betty's cheeks, and she kept repeating that it was all her fault. We tried to comfort her, but to no avail. Carrie looked sick, too, and I knew she blamed herself.

Worried, we all sat quietly, waiting for the police to come to talk to us.

It was at least half an hour before Lieutenant Belmont arrived. We wouldn't have known he was on the scene except for Dave, who poked his head in and told us to stay where we were unless anybody needed to use the downstairs powder room. He said the lieutenant would be in soon because he wanted to talk to the witnesses himself.

A few minutes later, he arrived with a young officer in tow. Lieutenant Belmont was wearing a well-fitted navy suit. Since this was the second time lately I'd noticed that he'd made an effort to dress well, I couldn't help wondering what had inspired him to change his sloppy ways. There was no time to speculate about the reason for the dour detective's clothing choices, because as soon as he saw Susan and me, he rolled his eyes.

"Not you two, again," he growled.

Susan lost no time informing the lieutenant that she hadn't witnessed Monique's fall because she'd been in the library the whole time.

"Is that so?" he asked.

"Yes, that's so!" Since he'd once arrested Susan for a crime she hadn't committed, causing her to spend a horrible night in jail, she wasn't a fan of the grumpy detective.

"Susan wasn't outside when it happened," I confirmed.

"And I suppose *you* were."

"Yes."

"Figures." He turned to Susan. "You can go. Leave your number with Boyd here in case we have any questions later."

Susan wasted no time. She jumped up, spoke briefly to the uniformed cop who accompanied Lieutenant Belmont, and left the room.

The lieutenant sat down in the chair Susan had just vacated. He looked surprised when he sank into its plush seat. "Nice chair," he commented.

Now it was my turn to be surprised as the lieutenant seldom had anything good to say, and he wasn't inclined to offer compliments.

"Did all four of you see Monique d'Albert fall?" he asked.

"No, my grandmother and I didn't see anything," Carrie said.

"All right. You can give your particulars to Sergeant Boyd over there unless you have something pertinent to offer."

"This is our house—my grandmother's and mine," she informed the lieutenant, "and our party."

"In that case, I'll interview you separately, and I'll need a list of all the guests who were invited, along with a list of who actually attended and what they wore."

"Of course. I'll print out the guest list and put a check mark by everybody I know came. I can't say for sure what each guest wore. I only know some of them."

The lieutenant opened his mouth to say something, probably something nasty, but he restrained himself at the last second.

"Just do the best you can," he said wearily. "We'll piece it together after my officers have interviewed everybody."

"The guest list is on my computer upstairs. Is it all right to go up there now?"

"Yeah, Boyd here will go with you."

As Carrie and Betty left the room with Sergeant Boyd, they passed Chip who had just entered. He spotted us and came over.

"Dave said you wanted to talk to all the witnesses," Chip told the lieutenant.

"So all three of you saw what happened?"

"Yes, we did," Brian answered, "along with several other people who were outside on the patio at the time."

"OK, I want to hear from each one of you separately, but first write down the names of everyone who was outside and what they were wearing."

"There were a couple of people I didn't know," I said.

"That goes for me, too," Chip added.

"I didn't know most of them myself," Brian added.

"Here," the detective said, handing me a small notebook and pen. "Do your best."

While Brian and Chip looked on, I scribbled the names of all the people I could remember who'd been on the patio, along with a brief description of their costumes.

"Anybody to add, you two?" the lieutenant said to Brian and Chip, but they both shook their heads. "OK, take off for a few minutes, but stay in the room and no comparing notes, you guys. I'll talk to Mrs. Trent first."

It didn't take long for me to relate what I'd seen. I stuck to the facts, not adding that I was convinced Monique had been pushed until the very end of my story. The lieutenant dismissed me and called Chip over next.

Their voices were low at first, but after a few minutes, the lieutenant, clearly irritated, raised his.

"Baxter, why didn't you tell me you were Monique d'Albert's date?"

"I'm telling you now," Chip answered, equally incensed.

"That's not true!" Brooks called out. "*I* was Monique's date!"

Chapter 10

When Lieutenant Belmont saw that Brooks Miller was the man who'd protested, he attempted to rise from the plush chair where he was seated, but he'd sunk so low into the soft cushion that he struggled to get up. Finally succeeding after his ungainly effort, he confronted both men. "What's this all about?" the crochety detective demanded.

"Monique invited me to come to the party with her," Brooks explained. "I arranged for a chauffeur and a limo from the Resort to drop her off, and I was supposed to meet her here for her grand entrance and escort her up the red carpet. Unfortunately, I was unavoidably detained when I had to deal with some business at work. That's why I was late."

"She asked *me* to be her date right after Carrie invited her to the party," Chip said incredulously. "I don't get it."

"Were you angry with her when you arrived and found out she was with Baxter here?" Lieutenant Belmont asked Brooks.

"Don't be ridiculous! I never saw Monique," Brooks explained. "I was looking for her when I heard the sirens."

"Can anybody verify your whereabouts at the time?"

"What? You *suspect* me? I had no reason to harm Monique!"

"Sounds like she was two-timing you. I'll ask you again: where were you when Monique fell?"

"Like I said, I was looking around the house for her. Amanda saw me, didn't you?" Brooks turned toward me.

"Yes, you asked Susan and me if we'd seen Monique, and I told you she was upstairs in Carrie's studio."

"I looked in the studio. There were several people there, but not Monique. I asked Carrie where she'd gone, but she didn't know. She suggested maybe the powder room. I waited outside the restroom upstairs in the hallway, but when someone else came out, I went back downstairs to look for her. I know a lot of people saw me."

"All right, Mr. Miller; calm down."

"I don't appreciate being treated like a common criminal."

As the richest man in Lonesome Valley, Brooks wasn't without influence, and the lieutenant was well aware of that fact, which was undoubtedly why he'd been fairly restrained when he questioned Brooks. I was sure he didn't want to get any flack from the police chief about poor treatment of a local bigwig.

"Sir, I'm just doing my job," the detective said in a matter-of-fact tone, "and I can't do it without asking questions. A woman was seriously hurt here tonight."

"She wasn't just seriously hurt," Carrie cried, as she entered the room with Sergeant Boyd right behind her. "She didn't make it. She's dead!"

Chapter 11

Carrie began to sob, and I hurried to her and urged her to sit down. She was pale and shook uncontrollably as I eased her onto the sofa. From the shocked expressions on the guests' faces, I realized that they hadn't expected the worst.

The lieutenant glared at Sergeant Boyd.

"She heard me calling the hospital," Boyd said sheepishly, earning himself another scowl from the lieutenant, who shook his head as though he couldn't believe Boyd would have been so careless.

"We have a homicide investigation on our hands now," Lieutenant Belmont proclaimed. "Pass the word that I don't want anybody to leave here until they've told an officer where they were at the time of the incident and who was with them. Got it?"

"Yes, sir," Boyd ducked out of the room before the lieutenant had a chance to chastise him further.

In the meantime, I tried to comfort Carrie, but she was quite upset, still blaming herself for not concealing the keys to the third floor rooms. When she'd calmed down a bit, I asked her where Betty was.

"Upstairs in her bedroom," Carrie sniffed. "She's absolutely devastated. She blames herself for what happened, but I should have known enough to put those keys away."

"It's not your fault, Carrie. You didn't push Monique off the balcony."

"No, but she should never have been able to get into that room."

"I think she knew she wasn't supposed to go up there. After all, Betty had roped off both stairways to the third floor."

Carrie moaned, and I supposed she was inconsolable at the moment, but I hoped she'd come to realize that she shouldn't blame herself for Monique's death. Whoever pushed her was to blame.

While I was with Carrie, the lieutenant had talked with Brian and Chip, and now he was beckoning me to come over again. Our conversation turned out to be brief because all he did was ask me to confirm what I'd told him earlier. Since I'd already recounted exactly what I'd seen, I was sure my account was the same as Brian's and Chip's because he just nodded as he flipped through his notes and then dismissed me.

"He said we could leave now," I told Brian when I joined him.

As we headed down the hallway, toward the entryway, we bumped into Dawn and Dave.

"Oh, I'm glad I caught you," Dave said. "Would you mind giving Dawn a ride home? I'll be here for hours yet, but there's no need for her to hang around."

"Sure, we'd be happy to," Brian said.

"Great. I'll walk outside with you. I could do with a breath of air."

As soon as the four of us went out, onto the front porch, the chill of the night air made me shiver, and Brian put his arm around me.

"Good thing my heater starts right up," he said. "We'll have you warmed up in no time."

We were walking down the front sidewalk when we heard a call.

"Over here! Over here!" Carrie's neighbor Patricia across the street gestured for Dave to come over.

We all trooped across the street to find out what she wanted.

"Are you a real cop or is that outfit just a Halloween costume?"

"I'm a police sergeant," Dave replied.

"Then I need to tell you that I saw something up there, right before that poor woman went over the railing. I just happened to glance out my front window, and I wasn't wearing my glasses at the time, so it was all a little blurry, but I think I saw a flash of red before she fell through the railing."

"When you say 'flash of red,' do you mean something like a flashing light?"

"No, not like that. I just had the very quick impression of a red color, maybe part of a costume? But the woman who fell wore pink. She's the one who arrived in a limo, isn't she?"

"Yes."

"I saw her parading up the sidewalk in her pink gown. Of course, I had my glasses on then. Betty told me to be sure to watch her front door if I wanted to see the guests arriving in their costumes." Patricia paused for a moment, as though switching gears. "I saw the ambulance come and go. Have you heard how the poor girl's doing?"

"Unfortunately, she didn't survive," Dave told Patricia.

"Ah, I was afraid of that. How awful! Betty and Carrie must be beside themselves."

"Yes, they're very upset. Did you happen to notice anything else?"

"Not really. I mean, I saw a man in a Dracula costume leave to go to his car right after the ambulance arrived. He was parked about half a block up."

"How could you tell without your glasses?"

"Oh, I had them on by then. I ran to get them after I saw the lady fall."

"All right. Anything else?"

"He pulled out into the street and waited until the ambulance took off. Then he followed it."

"That couldn't have been Brooks," I said. "He's still in the library. It must have been that other guy dressed as Dracula."

Dave frowned. "You don't happen to know who he is, do you, Amanda?"

"Susan and I both saw him; so did Brooks, but no, I didn't recognize him, and neither did they. The guy was wearing one of those half-masks; you know, like Zorro."

"OK, well, it sounds as though he may have turned up at the hospital. I'll check on that later. I need to get some more information from Mrs. . . . ?"

"Salazar. Patricia Salazar."

"Mrs. Salazar," Dave confirmed. He turned to us. "There's no need for any of you to wait."

He gave Dawn a quick peck on the cheek. "I'll see you at home later, honey. Tell your mom thanks for babysitting."

"I will. 'Bye now."

I'd intended to ask Dawn whether her mother Dorothy had worn the Little Red Riding Hood costume to the party, but in all the excitement I'd spaced it. Now I didn't have to ask, though, because Dorothy hadn't attended the party. Now I wondered why she'd skipped an event that almost all the other members of the Roadrunner had attended.

When we were all settled in Brian's car with the heater blasting warm air, I gave in to my curiosity.

"I thought your mom was going to come to the party," I said to Dawn. "Did you have a problem getting a babysitter?"

"No, we have several neighbors who babysit for us sometimes, although Mom usually does it if she's free. She didn't want to attend the party. Unfortunately, she had a situation with Betty a couple of years ago that pretty much ended their friendship. Betty had signed up for one of Mom's hand-throwing pottery classes, but during the third lesson, she got so frustrated that she threw her clay on the floor. Mom tried to explain that nobody gets it perfect right away. Like any skill, throwing a pot takes practice, loads of practice. We always tell the students not to put pressure on themselves. Nobody's going to become a great ceramist overnight.

"Anyway, class is supposed to be fun, but Betty wanted her money back. When she demanded a refund for the class fee, Mom stuck to our policy of no refunds after a class has already started. Of course, their discussion took place in front of everybody else in class, so the whole incident was quite disruptive. Betty left in a huff, and the two haven't spoken since."

"Wow, I had no idea."

"It's a shame. I'm afraid Betty just couldn't relax enough to have fun working with clay. She's kind of a perfectionist."

"I got that impression, too, when she blamed herself for leaving the keys right where she and Carrie normally keep them. She couldn't possibly have anticipated that Monique would take them and go up to the cupola. By the way, did you happen to see the woman who was wearing the Red Riding Hood costume at the party? When Patricia mentioned that she saw something red, I thought about her. She had the reddest costume I've ever seen."

"You know, I did see her walk through the living room, but I wasn't close enough to talk to her. I did notice that she wore one of those full face masks. It kind of looked like a doll's face."

"That's definitely the same woman I saw. I wonder who she was."

"I'll be sure to mention her to Dave, so they can figure out who it was. I know they'll be taking a close look at everybody who wore red, present company excepted, of course."

"Of course," Brian said, patting his red and black plaid shirt. "I guess I have an air-tight alibi since we were outside when Monique was pushed off the balcony."

"So horrible! And unbelievable, too! I know she irritated a lot of people with her constant flirting, but I don't think she was really serious about it. It was just her way. I can't imagine that someone would push her to her death because of that."

"I know. That does seem like a stretch, although I guess it's possible," I said, remembering how upset Valerie had been the first time Frank had ignored her in favor of Monique. Perhaps she had been even more hurt when it had occurred a second time. At least, I assumed so; since Susan and I had never located either Valerie or Frank when we went looking for them at the party, I didn't really know what had happened between them. I did know one thing, though: they'd both been wearing red berets.

Chapter 12

Images of every guest I'd seen at Carrie's party who wore red swirled in my mind until I finally fell asleep sometime in the early hours of the morning. When my eager dog bounced up to wake me early, as usual, I moaned, rolled over, and went back to sleep. Laddie must have given up for a while, but around seven thirty, he began patting me with his paw.

"OK, Laddie; Mommy's getting up now."

Brian and I had agreed to meet at eight to take Laddie for a walk to the neighborhood park, so I had just enough time to dress and have a cup of strong tea before it would be time to go.

When I went into the kitchen to put the kettle on, I was surprised to find Emma already awake and tapping away on her laptop.

"Aren't you and Matt going out this morning?" I asked. They normally breakfasted at their favorite restaurant on Sunday morning, even if one or both of them were scheduled to work at the feed store because it didn't open until eleven on Sundays.

"No, Mom, I have a ten-page research paper due tomorrow, and I just started it. It's going to take me all day and maybe half the night to write it."

"Oh, Emma," I sighed. Unfortunately, my daughter seemed to have inherited my procrastination gene. This wasn't the first time she'd done a major assignment at the last minute, but, so far, she'd always managed to come through. "You might need some fuel for those brain cells. How about some bacon and eggs?"

"No, thanks. I already had some cereal," she said, without taking her eyes off her laptop.

"All right. I'll leave you to it. Brian and I are taking Laddie to the park in a few minutes."

Totally absorbed in her project, Emma nodded but didn't look up. I felt a little guilty because Emma had often observed that I put things off. I shook my head, wondering whether our bad habit was hereditary or environmental.

I had just enough time to drink my tea before Brian knocked on the door of the studio. Raring to go, Laddie raced to the door and panted in anticipation as Brian patted him and I slipped his collar on with the leash already attached.

The morning air was nippy, and Brian and I both wore winter jackets and knit caps, but Laddie loved the cold, and he pranced along happily. Of course, he had his very own double fur coat. We set off at a brisk pace but slowed to a more leisurely one once we reached the park where there were several other dog walkers. Each time we greeted them, Laddie greeted their dogs. We were about halfway around the park when we spotted Rebecca and Greg Winter coming toward us with their little terriers Skippy and Tucker. Belle and I had met the couple at this very park a few months after I'd moved to Lonesome Valley, and we'd become friends.

Greg, who'd always been very concerned with safety and security, didn't waste any time asking us whether we'd heard about the murder last night. When he found out we'd seen Monique fall, he was so upset that Rebecca urged him to sit down on one of the park benches.

"Calm down, Greg," Rebecca said, as he clutched his chest. "You'd better take one of your pills."

Greg had been diagnosed with angina several months earlier. He reached into his pocket, shook a pill out of a small prescription bottle, popped it into his mouth, and held it under his tongue. After a couple of minutes, he muttered that he was all right and stood up.

"We knew her, you know," Greg said.

"Monique?"

"Yeah, but she wasn't Monique d'Albert back when she was in high school, just plain Mona Albert. She and our daughter ran around with the same crowd."

"Mona was a very popular girl," Rebecca said.

"Too popular for her own good, you mean," her husband added. "Remember the time when she was caught kissing the art teacher?"

"Not Frank, I hope," I said.

"His name was Kevin Stark, I believe. And her story was that *he* kissed her, not the other way around," Rebecca recounted. "In any case, he was the adult, and she was a teenager, so he was supposed to be the responsible one. The school board members were all outraged, so they fired him, and he left town. I don't know whatever became of him. After the girls graduated, we didn't see much of Mona, although we'd bump into her around town occasionally. I was flabbergasted when I heard she'd married that billionaire."

"I'm surprised she came back to Lonesome Valley after he died," Greg added. "She didn't even get along with her own cousin very well."

"I remember," Rebecca nodded. "I can't think of the girl's name, but she destroyed some of Mona's art portfolio in her senior year. The two of them were always squabbling over something, usually boys, I think."

"Well, that's another reason that it's strange she decided to come back here to live. There was always some drama with other girls who thought Mona was trying to steal their boyfriends." Greg said. "Now I don't know what happened or who she set off, but if she'd stayed in California, maybe she'd still be alive. Honestly, I don't know what this town is coming to. We didn't used to have any serious crime around here, but now, it's just terrible. A person can't even be safe with a big group of people around. I heard there were at least sixty people at that party last night."

"Unfortunately, the wrong person was there, too," Brian commented. "The police have no idea who pushed Monique off the balcony."

"I'll bet Amanda has some ideas," Rebecca said.

"Don't encourage her," Greg told his wife. "She could put herself in danger if she starts snooping around."

"Hello, I'm right here," I said.

"Sorry, Amanda, but you have to admit, you've been in some sticky situations this past year. Better let the police find the killer. If you try to investigate, the killer might go after *you*."

"I appreciate your concern, Greg, but I'm not investigating," I protested. "I already told Lieutenant Belmont everything I know, which wasn't much, and so did Brian."

Brian jumped in and asked Rebecca whether they were planning on taking Skippy and Tucker to the canine costume parade next Sunday. As it turned out, they were, so we told them we'd see them there and continued on our way.

"Thanks for changing the subject," I said to Brian after we were out of earshot. "You saved me from a lecture. Greg's a nice man, but he tends to go overboard sometimes."

"So you're not going to look into the murder?"

"I can't help thinking about it, I guess, but we certainly don't have any more insight into what happened than the police do. In fact, they probably know a lot more than we do because they interviewed everybody at the party. By now, they should have figured out which guests have others who can vouch for their whereabouts at the time of the murder and which ones don't. I *am* curious about Little Red Riding Hood, though. I wonder who she could be. You didn't happen to see her at the party, did you?"

"No, can't say that I did. I must have been in the library when you saw her."

"Well, let's hope the police can find out. We'd better get back. I need to change before we go to brunch with Belle and Dennis."

"So do I. I suppose I shouldn't wear jeans to the fanciest restaurant at the Resort."

"I'm sure some of the customers do, but it's fun to dress up once in a while."

"Yeah, fun," Brian replied, less than enthusiastically, and we both laughed.

When we returned, Brian and I went our separate ways to get ready, and I found Emma still hard at work. I offered to make her a pot of coffee before I jumped into the shower.

"Thanks, Mom. That would be great!" she said, without looking up from her laptop.

Laddie trailed me into the bedroom and waited while I got ready for the elegant champagne brunch that the four of us would soon be enjoying. My golden boy sensed something was up, and he didn't want to leave my side.

Tail wagging furiously, Laddie accompanied me to the door when Brian knocked, and he crowded in for all the attention he could get before we departed, leaving him with Emma, who'd be too busy to play with him, and his feline roommate, who would have preferred that he leave with us. What he didn't know was that when we returned, we planned to take him for a hike along a trail in the foothills. He would definitely love his long walk, but, in the meantime, I knew he'd settle down and take a nap after we left.

Belle's car was already parked in the driveway as Belle and Dennis came out of their house. Brian and I climbed into the back, and Dennis held the passenger door for Belle before jumping in behind the wheel.

As soon as we were off, Belle turned around to ask me whether I'd seen the morning news.

When I told her I hadn't, she said, "Lonesome Valley made the national news, and not in a good way. Everybody was talking about Monique d'Albert's murder and speculating about whether or not it may have had anything to do with her husband's death and the legal battle with his daughter over his estate. I bet reporters will be all over town before we know it."

"I hadn't thought about that, but you're right. If it's a national story, I suppose they'll be swarming."

"The cops aren't going to be too pleased," Brian commented. "Just think of all the pressure they're going to be getting to solve the case."

"That's for sure," I agreed. I couldn't help remembering that the chief's insistence on an arrest was the reason Pamela had initially been charged with the murder of her husband, although, thankfully, the guilty party was now in jail, awaiting trial.

"Bill Belmont's going to be at his wit's end. Couldn't happen to a nicer guy," Dennis, who'd voted to throw the grouchy lieutenant out of a photography club, added. Like Susan, Dennis wasn't a fan of the lieutenant. I'd been able to work with him a few times, and I knew he wasn't all bad, but he certainly lived up to his reputation as a curmudgeon.

When we arrived at the Resort, Belle's prediction was confirmed. We saw several satellite trucks from various news organizations in the parking lot, and when we passed the reception area on our way to the restaurant, I spotted a well-known reporter from one of the major news networks.

We walked down the mall but didn't pause to look into shop windows since we were in a hurry, arriving at the restaurant with only a couple minutes to spare before our reservation. We didn't have to wait long before the host appeared, showed us to our table in a lovely little alcove, and left us perusing the gorgeous, but pricey, brunch menu. While we pondered our choices, the wait staff filled our water glasses and coffee cups and poured us each a glass of champagne.

Our server materialized just as we'd all decided on our selections. Brian and Dennis both ordered ribeye steak with truffled puree while

Belle and I opted for sweeter choices—stuffed berry and ricotta French toast with maple syrup for Belle and pumpkin pancakes with cream cheese syrup for me.

"This restaurant certainly lives up to its reputation," Brian said when we'd finished our meals.

"Hear, hear," Dennis agreed.

"We'll have to come again sometime," Belle said. "What do you think, Amanda?"

"I'll make it unanimous."

"I'm glad the place turned out to be as good as the food critics said," Brian commented. "I've been to a few restaurants that were hyped, but they were nothing special."

"Maybe the restaurants' managers knew the critics were in the house and catered to them especially," Belle suggested.

"I wouldn't doubt that a bit," Brian agreed. "Sure would explain the difference between the reviews I read in the paper and the food I ordered."

As we strolled through the mall on our way back to the car, we paused occasionally to window shop, since there was no need to rush now. Dennis spotted a turquoise bolo tie in a Western wear shop that he wanted to look at, so we all agreed to meet at the entrance in twenty minutes. Then, he and Belle went into the store to check it out while Brian and I continued strolling along the mall. As we were gazing at a boutique's display, I caught a whiff of an unmistakable spicy scent as someone walked past us. I turned to see a tall man striding down the mall. He was already a few yards ahead of us when I spotted him.

Grabbing Brian's arm, I pointed out the guy. "I think that's the other man who was wearing the Dracula costume last night! Let's see if we can catch up to him."

Before Brian had a chance to answer, Brooks came out of his art gallery and bumped into the guy, and we hurriedly walked their way.

"Excuse me, sir. I didn't see you coming," Brooks apologized.

"No harm done," the man replied.

"Say, didn't I see you at the party last night?" Brooks asked. "You were wearing a mask, but. . ."

For a moment, I thought the man would deny it.

"You were Count Dracula," I piped up.

"And you wore a Victorian bathing outfit," he said. "Look, I suppose you folks want to know what I was doing there since I'm not a member of the Roadrunner."

"I certainly do," Brooks stated flatly. "You acted as though you were trying to avoid me when I ran into you on the stairs last night. Who are you, anyway?"

"I'm Todd Whitman, Monique's lawyer. I came out here from Palm Springs a few days ago. She invited me to the party. She asked me to meet her there."

Chapter 13

"Not you, too," I blurted out.

"Let's go inside the gallery," Brooks suggested. "It's too crowded out here in the mall, and we're blocking the shoppers."

We all stepped inside, where I feasted my eyes on the vibrant oil paintings displayed in the gallery's current exhibit. As usual, all the members of the Roadrunner had been invited to the opening, but I'd been in Florida visiting my parents at the time and hadn't had the chance to see it yet.

I promised myself I'd come back to get a good look some other time. Right now, I wanted to hear what this Dracula had to say. Only one couple was browsing, accompanied by a salesperson, so, after a round of brief introductions, Brooks led us to a quiet corner where we could talk.

"What did you mean by your remark, 'not you, too.'?"

"I'm sorry, Mr. Whitman, but it appears that you were one of three men Monique asked to the party. I wonder why she did that."

Todd Whitman didn't look especially shocked at this news. He shrugged, "Monique had her own way of doing things. She wanted to please people."

"You mean *men*," Brooks said. "She wanted to please men, and I fell for her flattery again, just like I did when we first dated a few years ago." The bitterness in his tone was unmistakable.

"You dated Monique?" Todd's surprise registered in his voice.

"I was about to ask her to marry me when she ran off with Edward McCall," Brooks revealed. As he stared at the floor, I wondered whether he was starting to wise up when it came to the women in his life, both of whom he'd chosen for their looks. His brief marriage had ended when his very unpleasant, but beautiful, wife had announced that she was bored with their life together. No one could accuse Monique of being unpleasant, though. At least, the two women didn't have that trait in common.

"So, my rival would have thrown in the towel if Monique hadn't died?"

"If I'd known then that she'd invited three men to the party, I would have," Brooks admitted.

"Sounds like you were hoping to be more than Monique's lawyer," Brian said to Todd.

"You're right. I'd asked her to marry me, but she put me off. Said it was too soon after her husband's death to even consider it."

"She didn't turn you down, though," Brian said.

"No, I'm sure she would have accepted my proposal at some point, maybe after she'd come to realize that she couldn't win her lawsuit."

"Why did you take her case then?" I asked.

"I was in love with her. I figured I'd be able to make her see the light eventually. There really wasn't any lawsuit, though, just a lot of public relations smoke."

"Do you mean there wasn't another will?"

"Oh, there was another will, all right, but it wasn't witnessed, and it wasn't in McCall's own handwriting. That will wouldn't have stood up in court, and I never actually filed suit. I was hoping to make enough noise that McCall's daughter would offer Monique some kind of settlement just to encourage her to go away. Monique had very little money of her own. She had plenty of credit cards that were all canceled after McCall's death, but not much in the way of liquid funds. Really, it was terribly neglectful of McCall not to provide for his wife. I may not be a billionaire, but I earn a good living. I could have taken care of her." Todd ended his statement with a sob. "I'm going to stay in Lonesome Valley until after Monique's memorial service. Monique didn't have anyone else, so I intend to make the final arrangements as soon as the coroner releases the body. I've been in contact with the police, but they're not able to tell me when I can proceed with the arrangements yet."

"That's generous of you, Whitman," Brooks said. "Let me know if there's anything I can do to help."

When Todd nodded, Brooks turned and left the gallery.

"Do you think he was still hung up on Monique?" Todd asked me.

"I wouldn't be surprised," I said before changing the subject. "You mentioned that Monique had no one else, but I believe she has a cousin who lives here in town."

"Really? Who is it?"

"If I remember right, her first name is Faye. I don't know her last name, though, but I could probably find out."

"If you can put me in touch, I'd appreciate it."

"I'll see what I can find out and let you know. Are you staying here at the Resort?"

"Yes, but there's no need to go through the switchboard." he said, "Just call me on my cell phone."

"All right," I agreed, and we exchanged numbers.

"Thanks for your help." He said before he turned and left the gallery while Brian and I lingered for a few moments so that I could look at the wonderful artwork in the exhibit.

"People will be looking at *your* exhibit in a few months," Brian reminded me.

"Well, mine and four other artists'."

"Don't sell yourself short. It's a great accomplishment to be part of an exhibit at Ian's gallery. I'm sure a lot of your paintings will be flying out the gallery's door, and your name recognition should soar, too."

"Thanks for your encouragement, Brian. I just hope I can complete my new work in time."

"You will!"

"I'm certainly going to try, but my schedule does allow some time off, speaking of which: shall we go meet Belle and Dennis and head home to pick up Laddie?"

"Sure, I know he'll be happy to walk the trail."

"He'll be happy for some company, too. Emma's so busy writing her paper that she doesn't have time to play with him today."

Despite my promise to find out Faye's last name and let Todd know, I wanted to enjoy the afternoon, so I waited until after we'd taken Laddie for his hike and Brian had headed back to work in southern Arizona before I made any calls to research Monique's cousin. As far as I could remember, Chip, Susan, and Pamela had all been in the gallery when Faye had shown up to tell Monique off. Under the circumstances, I wondered whether Faye would want to have any input into the final arrangements for Monique since she was so furious with her the last time they'd seen each other. At least, I assumed it had been the last time. For all I knew, they could have made up later, but, somehow, I doubted it.

After checking with Chip and Susan, I found out that neither knew Faye's last name. Although I was fairly certain that Monique had never mentioned it, I called Pamela just in case she knew. When she didn't answer, I decided to check with her in the morning.

In the meantime, I went into the studio, got out my laptop, and set it on top of my desk. Laddie insisted on putting his head on my lap, and he was so cute, I couldn't deny him, so I petted him with my left hand while tapping on the keyboard with my right hand.

Checking Monique's social media profiles, I hoped to locate Faye and then find her profiles, but the only trace of her was one photo of the two cousins together, but it wasn't captioned or tagged.

I was about to give up for the evening when it occurred to me that Brooks might know. He'd already left before I told Todd that Monique had a cousin who lived in town, so he couldn't know that Todd wanted to contact her.

Brooks answered right away when I phoned him. I explained that Todd wanted to contact Monique's cousin and asked him whether or not he knew Faye's last name.

"Faye. I remember meeting her a few times when Monique and I were dating, but I don't remember her last name. Maybe the police would know. I would imagine they make every effort to notify next-of-kin when there's a homicide."

"You're right. I don't know why I didn't think of that. I'll check with Dave Martinez." I paused. "Were Monique and her cousin close?"

"Not especially, from what I observed, which was a little strange, considering that those two were the only family they had left. They did keep in touch, though, at least back when Monique and I were dating."

"What happened to the rest of the family?"

"They'd all been vacationing together somewhere near a lake in Colorado, and the cabin where they were staying literally exploded. Monique and Faye had gone into town to go to a movie, so they weren't there, but everybody else had stayed at the cabin. Apparently, there had been a gas leak, but the family must have been asleep, I suppose."

"How horrible! You'd think they would have been especially close after going through the trauma of losing their families in such a terrible accident."

"Maybe it had the opposite effect. Monique never talked about the explosion much, but she told me she felt guilty for not being in the cabin with the rest of the family at the time. She said it had been her idea to go to the movies, so maybe Faye somehow blamed her. I don't know. I'm just guessing. You never really know what goes through other people's minds, do you?"

"No, I suppose not."

After I hung up, I went to the kitchen to brew a cup of herbal tea and found Emma rummaging through the refrigerator.

"I see you've come up for air."

"Yes. I'm starving. I've hardly eaten all day."

"Why don't you sit down and relax for a few minutes while I fix you some dinner."

"OK. Thanks, Mom! That'd be great."

"Hmm," I said as I peered into the fridge. "It looks as though a trip to the grocery store is in order, but we have eggs and cheese. How about an omelet and some toast?"

"That's fine."

"How's the paper coming?" I asked her, as I cracked the eggs.

"It's getting there. I should be finished in a couple of hours."

"I'm glad you won't have to stay up all night to work on it."

"Me, too!"

As Emma and I chatted, Laddie sat watching us, his head turning back and forth as we each spoke. Mona Lisa crept out from behind the sofa, where she'd been hiding, and wound her way around Emma's ankles before curling up with her head on Emma's foot.

When Emma resumed work on her paper, I took Laddie outside for one last time before we went to bed. As he wandered around the yard, checking the perimeter, I thought about poor Monique, the family tragedy she'd endured, and her own death.

I was beginning to understand that there was more to Monique that the flirty persona she'd been known for. Monique had been a complex individual with more than one side to her, although her marriage to Edward McCall, as well as her dating Brooks, certainly seemed to indicate that she'd been interested in marrying for money. That strategy hadn't worked out too well since her husband hadn't left her any. She'd also seemed truly interested in advancing her career as an artist, as indicated by her plans to open her own gallery in Palm Springs. Her husband's death had ended those plans, but she'd rejoined the Roadrunner as soon as she'd moved back to Lonesome Valley.

I couldn't imagine that anyone would have had a strong motive for killing her, not even her step-daughter, who'd inherited McCall's estate. However, since Monique had been pushed off the cupola's balcony to her death, there was obviously one person who wanted her dead.

According to Carrie's neighbor Patricia, that person had worn red. I asked myself how many people at the party fit the bill. Since Valerie and Frank had been wearing red berets, they both did. Then, there was the unknown woman who'd worn the Red Riding Hood costume. I wondered whether the police had been able to determine who she was. Of course, Brian had been wearing a red-and-black plaid shirt, but he was a witness, not a suspect. Although there could have been other people who'd worn red, I'd noticed only two others. Brooks and Todd had both worn Dracula costumes. Although their costumes weren't exactly alike, the two men had each worn a black cape with a red satin lining.

Chapter 14

After deciding that I'd check with Pamela and Dave Martinez to find out whether they knew Faye's last name, I spent a quiet evening with my daughter and pets, and I woke at least refreshed enough to face the day, if not embrace it wholeheartedly.

I waited until Emma and Matt left to drive to Flagstaff for their morning classes before taking Laddie for his walk and then brewing a pot of tea. I fixed a piece of cinnamon toast, poured a cup of tea, and turned on the television to catch the morning news. Monique's untimely death had made national headlines, but, oddly, the focus of the story was the feud between Monique and Edward McCall's daughter over the billionaire's vast estate, rather than the fact that Monique had been murdered.

I glanced at the time and realized it was probably still too early to call Pamela or Dave, so after downing my tea and finishing my toast, I worked on one of my new paintings for an hour or so while Laddie had a morning snooze on his bed in my studio and Mona Lisa retreated to the haven of her kitty tree for her own nap.

As I was squeezing a dab of burnt sienna onto my palette, my cell phone rang. I set the tube of oil paint down and picked up my phone.

"Hi, Pamela, I was going to call *you* later."

"Amanda, I'm sorry to disturb you. I bet you're painting right now, aren't you?"

"Yes, I am, but I can take a break. What's up?"

"I hate to ask you, but could you fill in for Carrie at the gallery for a couple of hours today? She has to leave at eleven, but she should be back around one. I've already called three other members, but, so far, no luck."

"Well, you're in luck now. Sure, I'll be there a little before eleven."

"Thanks, Amanda. You're a lifesaver. By the way, why were you going to call me?"

"Oh, I wanted to ask you if you know the last name of Monique's cousin Faye."

"The woman who kicked Monique out of her house?"

"Yes, she's the one."

"No, I didn't even remember her first name until you mentioned it just now. I hadn't ever seen her before she showed up at the Roadrunner last week. Why do you ask?"

"We ran into Monique's attorney at the Resort yesterday, and he said he wanted to organize her memorial service. When I mentioned she had a cousin, he told me he'd like to contact her to get her ideas about the service, so I volunteered to try to find out who she is."

"Maybe the police would know. Would you like me to ask Bill?"

So, Pamela now called Lieutenant Belmont "Bill." I didn't know anyone else, other than Dawn and Dave, who called the irascible detective by his first name.

"No, that's all right. I'll give Dave a call right now, while I'm thinking about it. See you at eleven."

"Thanks again, Amanda!"

I figured I could get in another hour of painting before I needed to change clothes for my brief stint at the gallery, but before I lifted my brush, I needed to call Dave.

"Amanda, what can I do for you this bright, beautiful day?"

"You certainly sound chipper this morning."

"I have the day off, and Dawn and I are off to Phoenix in a few minutes. She has some business to take care of there—a nationally distributed ceramics supplier is interested in carrying her special glazes."

"That's great news, Dave. I didn't know she was planning to expand."

"Nothing's official yet, so it'd probably be a good idea to keep it under your hat until the deal is sealed, but she thinks that might happen today."

"Well, tell her I wish her all the luck in the world. Is Dorothy going with you?"

"No, she's teaching her regular classes today. Anyway, she says Dawn's the salesperson in the family."

"Well, I won't keep you but a minute. I'm trying to find out the last name of Monique's cousin Faye, so that she can help with the arrangements for Monique's memorial service, but, so far, nobody I've asked has known her last name. I was hoping maybe the police have been in contact?"

"Yes, we have. Actually she contacted us before we could get to her. She must have heard the story about Monique's death on the television. She was furious that we hadn't notified her, but we were still in the process of trying to locate relatives when she showed up at the station. Anyway, that's neither here nor there. Her last name is Stanhope. Department policy prevents me from giving out her personal information like her phone number or address, but you should be able to locate her fairly easily by searching for her name. I suppose that, technically, I shouldn't have even given you her name, but since it has to do with final arrangements. . . ."

"Thank you, Dave. I'll pass her name along to Monique's lawyer. He's going to set up the service, and he wants to involve Faye since she appears to be Monique's only living relative."

"I believe that's the case."

"Thanks again, and have a great day!"

I didn't waste any time texting Todd Whitman that Faye's last name was Stanhope before squeezing in another hour's work on my abstract landscape, after which I hurriedly changed out of my paint-spattered sweatshirt and jeans into a more presentable outfit and grabbed a lightweight jacket since the day was unusually cold for late October. After checking on Mona Lisa, who was hiding behind the sofa, and telling Laddie to "be a good boy," I headed to the gallery.

Neither Carrie nor Pamela was in the front when I arrived, but I could hear voices coming from Pamela's office, so I stowed my purse and packable jacket in a large drawer beneath the counter. Since there were no customers in the gallery, I decided to clean the glass jewelry display case.

As I was wiping the case, Carrie, already dressed in her down jacket and a knit cap, and Pamela emerged from the office.

"Hi, Amanda, thanks for filling in. I should be back in a couple of hours. See you later."

Carrie hurriedly departed, and I turned to Pamela, who was frowning.

"Everything OK, Pamela?"

"I'm worried about Carrie. She's really been through the mill the past few days."

"I know. Monique's death was horrible."

"It certainly was, and Carrie's father. . . ."

"What do you mean? Has he taken a turn for the worse?"

I knew Carrie's father, who had Alzheimer's, had been a resident at the Lonesome Valley Nursing Home for several months.

"Not exactly, but there was an incident at the nursing home Saturday afternoon, and Carrie felt she couldn't let him stay there, so she took him home and hired some nurses to stay with him around the clock. Now, she's made arrangements for him at Mountain Vista Memory Care, and she's due there by noon. She's going home to pick him up, but she's afraid he won't want to leave, even though she has a big, strong nurse to help. The whole situation's extremely stressful for Carrie, her father, and her grandmother."

"That's a shame. I had no idea Carrie's father was at the house during the party. She didn't mention a word about it on Saturday."

"She says she should have canceled the party, but I think that's hindsight talking. At the time, she didn't want to cancel because the party was due to start in a few hours, and she wasn't sure she'd be able to notify everyone in time. Besides, she didn't want to disappoint her friends; a lot of people went all out for their costumes, and they were looking forward to showing them off at the party."

"That's true, but I'm sure the guests would have understood if she had canceled."

"She keeps saying if only she'd canceled, Monique would still be alive now. She seems to feel responsible, just because it happened at her house."

"There's no way Carrie could have anticipated that someone meant Monique harm. If whoever it was hadn't had the opportunity to kill her there, that person could have done it someplace else."

"Yes, that's true. It seems like we're not safe anywhere anymore," Pamela said with a sob.

"Oh, Pamela," I sighed, putting my arm around her. I knew she was thinking about her husband, who'd been stabbed at a city park, certainly a place most people would consider safe.

"Sorry, Amanda." Pamela sniffed. "I'll never get over Rich's murder."

"Of course not."

"I'm trying to manage the best I can, but some days, I really feel as though I can't go on."

"Pamela, you're coping admirably, and I know it's terribly difficult. Rest assured that your friends are always here for you."

"Yes, and I don't know what I'd do without you and all the other members of the Roadrunner. The gallery and the members are what keep me going. I need to get a grip and concentrate on business. I have some paperwork to take care of, if you don't mind. Call me if it gets busy."

"I will," I said, although I doubted that there would be any need for Pamela to assist prospective customers on a Monday, which was probably our slowest day of the week this time of year. Not one person had come into the gallery since my arrival.

Just as I'd anticipated, time dragged on. After determining that the gallery had already been dusted, I re-arranged the jewelry display before checking my email on my phone. Finding nothing new, I idly scrolled through the Ian Adams Gallery website, smiling as I noticed that he was now featuring one of my abstract landscapes on the gallery's homepage. I loved seeing my work in such a prominent spot, but it reminded me that I still had a lot of work to do to get ready for the show. Instead, I was babysitting an empty Roadrunner. Although I understood the gallery's policy of always having two members staffing it during the hours we were open, at times like these it seemed unnecessary. With a sigh, I put my phone back into my purse and closed the drawer. It was half past twelve, and Carrie should be returning by one. I wandered over to the front window and looked out. Bracing themselves against a strong wind that had come up since I arrived, only a few shoppers were scurrying down the street. Just watching them made me shiver. I hoped the cold spell wouldn't last too long. As I continued to view the scene on Main Street, I saw Carrie drive up and snag a parking spot right in front of the Roadrunner.

"The wind's awful out there," she said as she entered the gallery. "Any sales while I was gone?"

"No, nobody's been in at all," I told her.

"Sorry you had to come in," Carrie said, taking off her jacket. She tucked her knit cap into the jacket's hood and laid it over the chair we kept in back of the counter.

"Pamela told me you moved your dad."

"I sure did. Those jerks at the Lonesome Valley Nursing Home should be ashamed of themselves. They're supposed to be taking care of their patients, not knocking them around. I admit Dad can be a handful, but they're supposed to be trained to work with dementia patients. Dad got upset and shoved one of the nurses, and the guy retaliated. He actually hit Dad so hard that he knocked him down. They were in the hallway at the time. If I hadn't come around the corner and seen it with my own eyes, I wouldn't have believed such treatment. Of course, I checked him out of there immediately. On our way out, the receptionist whispered to me that it wasn't the first time a patient had been hit."

"That's shocking," I said, taken aback.

"Yes, it's terrible, and I don't intend to let it go. I've reported the incident to the police, but the director of the home is denying it ever happened. I'm going to report it to the state regulators, too."

"It sounds as though the place should lose its license."

"I agree. Dad didn't want to leave home to go to the memory care center, but we've tried to keep him at home with round-the-clock nurses before, and he always managed to slip away from them and wander outside. When he narrowly missed being hit by a car right in front of the house, Gram and I knew we'd have to move him to a home. Of course, we thought they'd be better prepared to handle a dementia patient. The people at Mountain Vista Memory Care assured me that he'd be safe there, but I'm going to pop in at unexpected times to see what's going on. Gram and I used to visit him at the nursing home every day, but we always came at the same time. I can see now that having a regular schedule was a big mistake."

I was about to respond to Carrie when we were interrupted by the chime on the gallery's door. After I spun around to greet our prospective customer and saw who is was, I shook my head in disbelief.

Chapter 15

I wondered what *she* was doing here.

"Hello, ladies. I'd like to speak with the gallery's director."

"Certainly," I said, recovering from my surprise. "I'll go get her."

Leaving Faye with Carrie, who probably had no idea that the woman who'd just shown up was Monique's cousin, I went down the hallway, tapped a courtesy knock on Pamela's office door, and entered.

"Pamela, we have a visitor, and she's asking to see you. It's Monique's cousin Faye."

"The woman who had a meltdown here last week?"

"The very same."

"Hmm. I wonder what she wants," Pamela said. She rose from her office chair and followed me back into the gallery.

"How may I help you?" Pamela asked politely.

"I'm afraid I owe you an apology. I was really upset when I came into the gallery looking for Monique last week. I'm sorry I made a scene." Faye's demeanor couldn't have been more different than it had been on that occasion. I thought she appeared somewhat hesitant, if perhaps not sincerely contrite. "If I'd known then that we'd lose Monique. . . ." She trailed off as a tear trickled down her cheek.

"Ah, yes; you're her cousin, aren't you?" Pamela said.

"First and only cousin. We were really very close. I know it probably didn't look that way when I threw her suitcase into the gallery, but Monique had a way of making me crazy sometimes, the way she flirted outrageously with my husband. Honestly, I don't think she did it on purpose; I guess flirting just came naturally to her."

"How may I help?" Pamela asked again.

"I'm still so flustered about making the final arrangements for Monique, and I'm trying to remember everything that has to be done."

"Excuse me, but have you talked with Todd Whitman, Monique's lawyer, yet?" I interrupted. "He said he'd handle the arrangements, but he wanted to get your input."

She nodded. "Yes, I'm going to meet him at the funeral home tomorrow, but since I'm Monique's only living relative, I though I should check on her artwork."

"Would you like to take a look?" Pamela asked. "Let me show you where her pastels are displayed."

Faye followed Pamela around the divider, into the back of the gallery. I turned to Carrie and saw that she looked as though she might faint.

"Carrie, sit down. You don't look well."

"I'll be back," she said, before disappearing down the hallway to the meeting room.

Although I wasn't sure what had upset Carrie, I figured she was still blaming herself for Monique's death and couldn't bear to face Faye, who probably had no idea who Carrie was or that the ill-fated costume party had taken place at Carrie's house.

I'd been ready to leave when Carrie returned to the gallery, but it looked as though she might have to go home, which meant I'd probably end up covering for her for the rest of the day. I hadn't left Laddie with Belle because I hadn't expected to be gone long, but now I thought it might be a good idea to have her pick him up, especially since I didn't expect Emma to get home before I did if I had to stay the rest of the afternoon at the Roadrunner. My golden boy would be more than happy to spend it with his little buddy Mr. Big. I opened the drawer where I'd put my purse and rooted around in it until I found my phone. Then I called Belle, who said she'd pick up Laddie and bring him to her house. After I thanked her, I promised to keep her posted. As usual, she assured me that she was happy to help.

After I slipped my phone back into my purse and closed the drawer, I smiled to think how fortunate I was to have such a good friend living right next door to me. I knew she felt that same way about me, which made me feel even better.

Pamela and Faye were still in the back of the gallery, so I decided to check on Carrie. When I walked down the hall and peeked into the meeting room, I found her sitting at one of the tables, but the color had returned to her face.

"Are you feeling any better?" I asked.

"Yes, I'm all right. I about passed out when I heard that the woman Pamela's talking to is Monique's relative. I *really* don't want to see her. If she knew who I was, she might blame me for Monique's death. Heaven knows that I blame myself. We knew that balcony needed to be repaired. I feel so guilty, and I know Gram does, too. We got distracted with taking care of Dad, and we weren't nearly as careful as we should have been about keeping people away from the third floor. Dad was staying in one of the rooms up there with his nurse, so we especially didn't want him disturbed."

"That's perfectly understandable. Anyway, you couldn't possibly have anticipated what happened. The one to blame here is the person who pushed Monique off that balcony, not you or your grandmother."

Although Carrie nodded, I was almost certain that my words hadn't made much impact.

"I still don't want to face that woman, Amanda," she said. "I'm going to hide out in here until she leaves; that is, if you wouldn't mind staying a while."

"Of course I will. I'll let you know when she leaves."

"Thanks, Amanda. I appreciate your understanding."

I put my hand on her shoulder. "You've had a rough day. Just try to relax for a bit. Have you had lunch?"

"I guess not; come to think about it, I haven't eaten a thing all day."

"No wonder you were feeling faint. As soon as Faye leaves, I'll run next door and get you a sandwich. Actually, Pamela and I haven't had lunch yet, either. I'll check with her, and if she's not planning on going out, I'll take orders and pick up our food next door at the Coffee Klatsch."

"That sounds good. I hadn't even thought about lunch until now, but the Coffee Klatsch's Thanksgiving Dinner Sub would be fine."

"It sounds great to me, too. I haven't had one for a long time, so I think I'll get the same thing."

When I heard the Roadrunner's door close, I stopped raving about the sandwich and returned to the front of the gallery in time to see Faye leaving. When I suggested lunch to Pamela, she agreed, and decided on the Thanksgiving Dinner Sub, too.

"I'll grab us some paper plates from the office, and we can all eat in the meeting room. If nobody's in the front here, I can practically guarantee we'll have some customers pop in."

. We both laughed at that. I shrugged on my jacket, grabbed my purse and went next door to place our order. I knew it wouldn't take long because the lunch rush was over. Ten minutes later, I was back with our food, and we gathered at one of the tables in the meeting room.

It seemed that Carrie had told Pamela why she'd been hiding out, and Pamela was trying to convince her, just as I had tried earlier, that she shouldn't blame herself for Monique's death.

"I know you're right—both of you—but I still can't help feeling guilty. And I'm so worried about Dad, too! They'd better treat him right at this new place!" she said fiercely.

"I've heard good things about Mountain Vista Memory Care," Pamela said.

"At least, Dad's alive, but poor Monique. . . and poor Faye. Now she has nobody left."

"She has her husband," I said, but the moment I spoke, I wished I could take back my words, which would only serve to remind Pamela that her own husband was dead.

Pamela didn't react to my statement, though.

I quickly changed the subject. "Did Faye come in to make arrangements for Monique's pastels?" I asked Pamela.

"Yes, she actually wanted to take them home with her today, but I told her that Monique had paid her hanging fees through the end of the year, and we'd very likely sell several of them, especially with the holiday season coming up, so she agreed to leave them here until then. I didn't say anything to Faye, but I wonder if we need to hear from her estate's executor that it's all right to release the pastels to her."

"Good point," I said. "At least, now you'll have time to check with Todd Whitman."

"He's Monique's lawyer, right?"

"Yes, I guess I just assumed he's her executor, too, but maybe not. I can ask him if you'd like."

"Good. I do think we should be on firm legal ground here. After all, Monique's pastels are worth quite a bit of money. I don't know whether Faye realizes just how much, but maybe she does because she asked to look around the apartment upstairs where Monique stayed. I told her Monique hadn't left anything there, but I figured it wouldn't hurt to let her see it."

"What happened?" Carrie asked.

"Nothing, really. I unlocked the door for her, and we went in together. We glanced around the place, but Monique had taken all her things with her when she moved to the Resort. Faye looked at all the artwork on the walls, but, of course, none of it was Monique's"

"I wonder what she thought about Chip's mural," Carrie said. "It's so striking; it totally dominates the living room."

"That's for sure," I said, remembering the first time I'd seen the scene Chip had painted on the apartment's living room wall. The realistic mural of an Arizona mountain habitat covered an entire wall and formed a backdrop for a life-size bronze cougar that had been sculpted by the former gallery director.

Most of the Roadrunner's members agreed that Chip should focus on his strong suit—murals—rather than dabbling in so many different types of media and styles, but it had become obvious to me that his experimentation in many forms of art was a necessary part of finding his way as an artist. In his case, it might be taking longer than usual, and I knew a few artists who'd never gotten there, even after decades, but I didn't believe Chip would be one of them, despite his slow start and nonchalant approach to his art.

Thinking about Chip's artwork reminded me that I couldn't afford to spend too much time away from my studio, so, as soon as we finished our sandwiches, I headed home, determined not to let the rest of the day's light fade before I had a chance to do some more painting.

Chapter 16

Staying only a few minutes at Belle's when I picked up Laddie, I got back to work right after I played the feather game with Mona Lisa while Laddie sat by my side and watched. Uncharacteristically, Mona Lisa had run to the door to greet me when we came home, and I couldn't ignore her. After we'd played the game for a while, I stopped flicking the feather, and she jumped to the top of her kitty tree, turned around to look down at Laddie, and hissed at him. I sighed at the display of sibling rivalry, but there wasn't much I could do about it.

Laddie followed me into the studio and settled down on his bed for an afternoon nap. I knew he was tired after his play date with Mr. Big. Vowing to be extra careful not to smear any paint on myself, I didn't take the time to change my clothes but got right to work on my abstract landscape. Later, Laddie woke up from his nap, just as the light became a bit dimmer, and I had to stop for the day.

Emma called to let me know that Matt had to do some research at the university library, so they would be late getting home. Since they planned to stop for dinner before driving back to Lonesome Valley, I was on my own. I didn't feel too inspired to cook, and I decided to clear out my tiny refrigerator by eating leftovers for dinner. After I fed Laddie and Mona Lisa, I sat at the table and nibbled my food while

I scrolled through the email on my phone. Although I'd prepared myself a regular-size dinner out of habit, I soon realized that I really wasn't too hungry because the Thanksgiving Dinner Sub I'd eaten for lunch had more than satisfied my appetite. I wrapped the meal in foil and set it back into the refrigerator.

I had the nagging feeling that I'd forgotten something. Remembering that there were towels in the dryer, I folded them and put them away, but the laundry wasn't what had been nagging me. Finally, I remembered my promise to Pamela to check with Todd Whitman to find out whether or not he was Monique's executor.

When I called him, the phone rang several times, and I was about to hang up without leaving a message when he answered, sounding out of breath.

"Hi, Amanda; you caught me at the gym. Can I call you back in about an hour?"

"That's fine," I assured him.

I hadn't had time to set my phone down before Brian called, asking how my day had gone, and I gave him a brief rundown.

"How about *your* day?" I asked, almost reluctantly because, for the past few months, Brian's job hadn't been going nearly as well as it had when he'd first accepted his position as manager of a massive wind power facility in southern Arizona.

Fortunately, his answer surprised me.

"Fine. It's the first day in months that I haven't had to deal with multiple calls from a bunch of bigwigs at headquarters who don't know what they're doing. In fact, I didn't field a single call from the corporate office all day. I actually got to do my job without being second-guessed about every little detail."

"That's great! Maybe they're backing off."

"Maybe. I wouldn't count on anything. Most likely, they were tied up in a meeting all day, and tomorrow will turn out to be same-old, same-old."

"I hope not."

"Me, too. I get tired of being treated as though I were a clueless, incompetent manager."

I knew Brian had been thinking about finding another job, even though his current job was one he'd really wanted. I remembered how enthusiastic he'd been when he first told me about it, and I wished he could like his "dream job," as he'd once called it, as well again. If the constant pressure he'd been under didn't ease up, I was fairly certain he'd be calling a headhunter soon in search of different employment.

"Oh, well, no point moaning and groaning now," he said, "but a break was certainly a welcome relief."

After we'd talked for quite a while longer, my phone buzzed with an incoming call. I figured it was probably Todd Whitman, returning my call, but I didn't want to interrupt Brian, and it wasn't crucial that I find out whether or not Todd was Monique's executor immediately, so I let the call go to voicemail and made a mental note to call him back tomorrow.

After another half an hour or so, we finally ended our conversation, promising to talk again the next evening.

Later, Emma came home to such exuberant greetings from both Mona Lisa and Laddie that my besieged daughter could barely get in the door. Emma swooped up Mona Lisa, who was meowing loudly, and slowly inched her way forward while Laddie, begging to be petted, bounced up and down in front of her.

After Emma finally managed to make it to the sofa and sit down, Laddie promptly lay his head on her lap. Emma tried to cuddle Mona Lisa in her right arm while she stroked Laddie's head with her left hand, but my calico kitty wasn't about to tolerate divided attention, and she reached out her paw to bat Laddie on the nose. Fortunately, Emma pulled the jealous cat away just in time to avoid her bare claws raking across Laddie's nose.

"Hey, you," Emma said softly to Mona Lisa. "Don't be naughty."

I sat down in the lone armchair and called Laddie. He immediately jumped up and ran to me. Satisfied that she had Emma all to herself now, Mona Lisa shot a ha-ha-ha look at Laddie before curling up in Emma's lap with her back toward Laddie and me. Laddie was so busy basking in my attention that he didn't even notice.

"Looks like they're both happy now," Emma commented.

"I'd say so."

"Would it be OK if I borrow the car tomorrow? Dennis had to change the schedule at the feed store, so I'm going to work in the morning, but Matt isn't scheduled to come in until noon."

"Sure. I'm planning on spending the day in the studio. Today, I didn't get to work as long as I'd planned because I ended up having to cover for Carrie at the gallery for a few hours. I can't afford to procrastinate and miss too much studio time, or I won't have as many new paintings done for the show as Ian wants."

"You have plenty of time, though, right? I mean the show's not till February."

"I know, but three months will go by in a flash, especially with the holidays coming up soon."

"That's true. Remember the day we went into Ian's gallery to browse and he asked to see your artwork?"

"I sure do. I'll never forget it. If we hadn't stopped in Scottsdale after I picked you up for Christmas break last year, I might never have had the chance. This show's an even bigger opportunity, so I don't want to blow it."

"You won't, Mom. I think your art career's going great."

"Thanks for the vote of confidence, Emma. Sometimes, I still can't quite believe I'm actually making a living with my painting."

Our discussion turning to other topics, Emma and I talked for over an hour while our precious pets continued to lap up the love, and it wasn't until the following morning, after Emma left for work, that I remembered that I hadn't returned Todd Whitman's phone call.

Hoping that I wasn't about to engage in another round of phone tag, I called him and was glad he answered on the first ring.

"It's Amanda Trent, Todd. I'm sorry I missed your callback last night."

"No problem, Amanda."

"I'm calling on behalf of the Roadrunner because Faye came into the gallery yesterday and told Pamela Smith, our director, that she wants Monique's paintings. Pamela explained that Monique had paid to hang her pastels at the gallery through the end of the year and suggested that they leave them in place, and Faye agreed for now. After she left, Pamela decided we should really find out whether it's all right to give Faye the pastels. Are you handling her estate?"

"Yes, I'm Monique's executor. She left everything to her husband."

"Does that mean McCall's daughter would be entitled to Monique's artwork?"

"No, in the event that he didn't survive her, Monique's estate goes to worthy causes, at my discretion. Odd that she never mentioned her cousin Faye, but I'm inclined to believe it was an oversight on her part because the only reason she had me write that will was to tweak McCall into making a new will of his own in her favor."

"I guess that didn't work out too well."

"No, it didn't. Anyway, about the pastels at the gallery: I'll need to inventory them, so I'd appreciate it if the director could send me a list of the works on display at the Roadrunner, and I'll take it from there."

"So I guess Faye's out of luck."

"Not necessarily. I have considerable leeway in distributing Monique's property, but, for now, let's maintain the status quo and leave them in the gallery."

"I'm assuming they could be sold, as usual."

"Of course. I'll just need an accounting of any sales."

"Pamela always does the accounting and distributes funds from sales at the end of the month, anyway. I'll let her know to send Monique's monthly recap and check to you. Thanks for your help."

"Thanks for yours. I was going to drop by the Roadrunner today, but now I won't have to. My next stop is the funeral home. Faye and her husband are supposed to meet me there. I wish I could be anyplace else in the world, but we all want to celebrate Monique's life, unnaturally short though it was." Todd ended with a catch in his voice, and I couldn't help thinking how different Monique's life might have been if she'd married Brooks and stayed in Lonesome Valley instead of running off and marrying Edward McCall.

After telling me that he'd let me know when the service for Monique would be scheduled, he rang off. I texted Pamela to tell her that Todd was indeed Monique's executor, and since he'd have the final word on the distribution of Monique's pastels, the Roadrunner should remain their home for the time being.

Although I wondered how Faye would take the news, it was entirely possible that she would be able to have the pastels. After all, Todd had told me that he had "considerable discretion" in distributing what few assets Monique had, and he certainly seemed to be considering turning her artwork over to her cousin.

Chapter 17

With Emma at work, Mona Lisa curled up on the sofa, and Laddie flopped down on his bed in the studio, ready for his morning nap, I didn't delay my painting any longer, although I did set a pot of strong tea on my desk and took a few sips occasionally when I stood back to get a different perspective on my expressionistic landscape, which I thought was coming along nicely. I'd punctuated the predominant magenta and fuchsia colors with shades of green and yellow, which I mixed on my palette or sometimes on the canvas itself to make just the right complex hues.

My concentration wasn't broken until Emma came home from work, and I saw that it was twelve fifteen. I was surprised Laddie hadn't jumped up earlier and begged me for a game of fetch outside, but as soon as he heard the car pull into the driveway, he was up and running to the kitchen door to greet Emma.

I set my palette down and joined them, closing the studio door behind me. I didn't want my rambunctious dog to knock my easel over in case his excitement morphed into zoomies, when he ran around in circles and then all around the house at a frantic pace.

"How was work, Emma?"

"Oh, fine. The store wasn't too busy this morning, so I spent most of the time stocking shelves. Shall I fix us some sandwiches for lunch?"

"How about a pizza, instead?" I suggested. "We haven't had one for a while. If you're not too hungry to wait, that is."

"Sounds good to me. I'll call and order. Should we get a large veggie supreme?"

"Fine. I was about to say I'd make a salad, but I just remembered I had to throw out the rest of the spinach this morning because it was going bad, so let's get a couple small salads, too."

"You got it," she said, picking up her phone.

Half an hour later I was in the backyard with Laddie when I heard the doorbell ring. By the time we went inside, Chip was handing the pizza and salads to Emma.

"Hi, Chip. You must be working the early shift today," I said as he reached down to pet Laddie.

"I'll be working until midnight. One of our drivers tripped and had a nasty fall yesterday, and now he's laid up with a sprained ankle, so yours truly will be doing double duty until he can get around without crutches."

"What a shame. I hope he recovers quickly."

"So do I. I went in with Dad at ten this morning to help prep for the day, and, by the time we clean up tonight, it'll make for a fifteen-hour day. I'm tired just thinking about it."

"I can imagine."

"Say, have the cops contacted you since Saturday night?"

"No, but remember when I called you to see if you knew Monique's cousin's last name?"

Chip nodded.

"Well, nobody I asked knew it, so I called Dave. He was able to give me Faye's last name, but he didn't ask *me* any questions."

"I bet Belmont will be in touch. He caught me at home this morning before Dad and I went to work. He wanted to know whether Monique had her cell phone with her at the party. When I told him I never saw it that evening, he grunted and left."

"Mr. Personality strikes again."

"Yeah. I can't believe Pamela puts up with him hanging around."

"He keeps her up to date on what's happening with Rich's homicide case, Chip. Anyway, he acts different when he's around her. She claims he's always been polite."

"Uh, huh. Doesn't sound like Belmont to me. Anyway, just thought that I'd give you a heads-up. I'd better get going." With a wave, he turned and jogged back to his car.

"See you later," I called.

Sure enough, Chip's prediction came true just a couple of hours later. I'd returned to my painting after lunch, and Emma had taken Laddie for a walk when the doorbell rang, startling me so much that I jerked the tube of paint I was squeezing, smearing a dab on my fingers. I picked up a cotton cloth and carried it with me, wiping my hands on it as I answered the door and invited Lieutenant Belmont to come inside.

He raised his eyebrows at my paint cloth and paint-spattered sweatshirt, but he didn't comment. Instead, he looked around and asked, "Where's the mutt?"

"My daughter took *Laddie* for a walk," I said, restraining myself. I didn't appreciate his rude comment, even though I knew he was deliberately trying to get under my skin. "I would have gone with them, but I have a ton of work to do."

"Uh, OK, I won't keep you long," he said. "Did you see Monique with a cell phone at any time on Saturday?"

"No, the first time I saw her was when she arrived in her Marilyn Monroe dress. She wasn't holding a phone, and there was no place she could have kept it in that dress."

"No pockets?"

I looked at him in astonishment. "You've got to be kidding."

"I assure you I'm not."

"You haven't seen the dress then. Let me show you a picture."

"I asked everybody to send me any photos or video they took at the party. How come you didn't do that?"

"I didn't take any pictures at the party, but I can show you a picture of the dress Monique was wearing. Sit down for a second. I need to grab my laptop from the studio."

Looking confused, he was sitting on the sofa, waiting for me, when I returned with my laptop open to a photo of Marilyn in the va-va-voom dress that Monique had copied.

"The dress Monique wore looked just like the original," I said, handing the lieutenant my laptop. "There's no place to hide anything in that dress."

"I see what you mean," he said. I wondered whether or not it was my imagination, but it looked to me as though the lieutenant was turning red.

"Monique must have left her phone in the limo," I guessed.

"Nope. We searched it and her suite at the resort. The chauffeur couldn't remember whether she had her phone with her or not."

"You think the killer got a hold of it, don't you? I bet you think Monique was lured to that cupola on Carrie's third floor."

"No comment."

Even though the lieutenant didn't confirm my suspicion, I could tell from the expression on his face that I was right.

"Do you have a suspect?"

"I think you know that we haven't announced any persons of interest."

"But that doesn't mean you don't have your sights set on someone, does it?"

"No comment."

As the lieutenant stood, the front door burst open, and Emma and Laddie came into the living room. When Laddie saw him, he immediately ran to the lieutenant, who awkwardly patted my golden boy's back and told him that he was a "good doggie."

"He likes you," I told the lieutenant.

Of course, my comment embarrassed the lieutenant, who clearly didn't know how to respond. He cleared his throat and patted Laddie a few more times. Before he left, he told me to let him know if I "stumbled onto anything."

On his way out, he nodded to Emma, who closed the door behind him.

"Did I hear the detective asking for your help?" she asked in amazement.

"I don't know. It kind of sounded like it. He usually tells me to mind my own business."

"You aren't investigating, are you, Mom? It could be dangerous."

"Not actively. I mean I've thought about who might have wanted to kill Monique, but that's as far as it goes. I've been concentrating on my painting, which I'd better get back to now."

My answer seemed to satisfy my daughter, and I returned to the studio with Laddie at my side and resumed painting while he lay down on his bed, yawned, and curled up with his tail wrapped around his snout.

As I switched from one brush to another, I thought about the theory that the killer had asked Monique to meet at the cupola. It certainly made some sense. Otherwise, I couldn't understand why she would climb the stairs to the third floor, especially since they were blocked off, at least symbolically, if not physically. Surely, she wouldn't just wander around the big house during a party. After all, she'd been the most popular guest there.

It was a wonder that she'd been able to be alone long enough to escape from her many admirers' sight, but since they hadn't followed her to Carrie's studio, she'd been able to slip out without anybody noticing. That had to have been when she made her way to the cupola, but, if so, I couldn't understand how she'd unlocked the door, which Carrie's grandmother had locked.

Then it hit me. Maybe Monique hadn't unlocked the door herself. Her murderer could have had the key and waited there for Monique to show up.

I didn't believe that Monique had feared she was in danger; otherwise, she wouldn't have gone upstairs, but her miscalculation turned out to be a fatal mistake.

Chapter 18

Although I couldn't believe it was mid-week already when Matt picked up Emma to drive to NAU for their morning classes, at least I felt less of a sense of panic than I had on Monday when Pamela had asked me to fill in for Carrie at the Roadrunner. Despite a few interruptions, I'd accomplished a great deal since then, and, even with the lunch break I was contemplating, I anticipated completing the landscape I'd been working on by late afternoon and beginning a new painting tomorrow.

Since Belle and I had barely had time to talk when I picked up Laddie from her house on Monday and I hadn't seen her at all yesterday, I called and asked her if she'd like to come over for coffee.

"How about bringing Laddie and coming over here at noon, instead. I know how busy you are, but we'll make do with a quick lunch. I have a new quiche recipe I want to try. How about it?"

"That sounds wonderful! We'll be there."

"I'll get going on my pastry crust, then. See you at noon."

Remembering to keep an eye on the time, I set to work on my painting and when I saw that it was a few minutes before twelve, I quickly exchanged my sweatshirt for a more presentable red cashmere sweater, snapped on Laddie's collar and leash, and exited the house without rousing Mona Lisa from her perch on her kitty tree.

"What a beautiful sweater!" Belle exclaimed after she opened the door.

"Thanks! My mom gave it to me for my birthday, but it was pretty warm then, so I've been saving it for cooler weather.

Laddie trembled with excitement at seeing his little buddy. Mr. Big was whipping around us in circles, and Laddie could barely hold still long enough for me to take off his leash. Then the two were off, playfully running and jumping around the house until Belle let them out, into the backyard.

"I'm almost ready. Could you keep an eye on the pups for a minute?"

"Sure." I stood at the patio door watching them while Belle cut the quiche and put a slice on each of our plates. She removed a large salad bowl and dressing from the refrigerator and set them on the kitchen table where she'd already poured tall glasses of iced tea at our places.

"All set," she announced. "You can let them in. I have a few salmon treats they can have."

As soon as Laddie and Mr. Big smelled the salmon bits, they gobbled them down and looked at Belle as if to beg for more.

"No more," she said, holding up up her empty hands. "Lie down now."

Laddie complied immediately, but Mr. Big continued to wiggle and bounce around. Unlike Laddie, he was too little to try to put his paws up on the kitchen table, so Belle suggested that he'd settle down if we ignored him, which we did, and he soon curled up next to Laddie.

"Mmm. This is good," I said, taking a bite of the quiche. "I don't think we've had it before."

"I usually make the traditional quiche Lorraine with the bacon bits, but I thought I'd go all veggie with artichokes and sun-dried tomatoes in this one, and I used Monterey Jack cheese instead of Gruyère. I had planned on making the crust from scratch, but I changed my mind, so I cheated with a frozen pie crust."

"Hardly a cheat! Pastry crusts can be so tricky, and they always take me a long time to roll out. This is a treat."

"I thought you probably needed a break about now."

"You're right. It helps to put the paintbrush down every once in a while. I've been worried about being able to complete all the new artwork in time for the show, but I'm starting to feel more confident. I can't afford to let up too much, but I'm planning to take some time off on the weekends."

"Will Brian be here for the pet parade on Sunday?"

"Yes, as far as we know at this point. He's had a couple of days now without any calls from his corporate offices, but you never know with those people."

I sighed. We'd had more than a few weekend plans canceled because company directors had descended unannounced on the facility Brian managed at the last minute.

"Let's keep our fingers crossed. I don't think either Dennis or Brian is too crazy about going to the pet parade with a bunch of dogs in their Halloween costumes, but I think it'll be fun. I just finished Laddie's lion outfit this morning, and Mr. Big's is ready, too."

"I can't wait to see them."

As soon as we were done with lunch, Belle called the dogs into her sewing room where their costumes awaited them. Laddie held still while Belle put his lion costume on him. She'd attached hook-and-loop fasteners so that the fluffy tan mane with the attached lion ears would be easy to adjust. Although the costume was fairly simple compared to others I'd seen, I thought Laddie looked quite lion-like.

"What do you think?" Belle asked.

"It's perfect! He looks so adorable."

While Laddie proudly pranced around the room, Belle picked up Mr. Big and struggled to hold the little dog still while she put his hot dog costume on him.

"He won't tolerate anything on his head, so I had to make him an outfit that could wrap around his body."

She set him on the floor and after a few attempts to nip at the side of the puffy bun of his hot dog costume, he gave up and trotted over to Laddie.

"How cute! I love the way you put squiggly mustard on the hot dog."

"It's just a yellow cord I bought at the fabric store, but I think it's a nice touch."

"We have to take pictures! Let's see if we can get them to pose."

Getting both dogs to sit still while we took their pictures proved to be a daunting task, but, after some maneuvering, we finally managed to get a few shots of the canines rocking their costumes, although they tended to wiggle or look the other way just as we were about to take a picture.

Our photo session over, Belle removed Mr. Big's costume, and we said good-bye. Laddie didn't seem to mind his lion outfit at all, so I left it on him until we got home. Then I returned to the studio for the rest of the afternoon while Laddie napped.

Finishing the detail work on my landscape came almost automatically to me, and I let my mind wander while I added the final touches to my painting. I asked myself why Lieutenant Belmont was searching for Monique's phone when I thought that the police had the capability to have the phone carrier track the device, but maybe that procedure didn't work if the phone was turned off. I didn't know whether just turning the phone off would prevent tracking or whether the battery needed to be removed, too. Maybe the phone had been destroyed by whoever had lured Monique to the cupola. Still, it was only a theory that someone had asked Monique to meet them at the cupola, but I thought that explanation for her ascending the stairs to the third floor at Carrie's certainly made the most sense. I could think of no reason that Monique would simply wander upstairs to go exploring.

Then there was the perplexing clue offered by Carrie's neighbor Patricia, who'd seen a flash of red before Monique crashed through the balcony rail. I knew of five people who fit the bill, but there could have been more, potentially many more, and since the police had collected descriptions of everyone's costume, Lieutenant Belmont was in a far better position to eliminate or tag them as suspects than I was.

Brooks and Todd Whitman both wore capes with a blood-red lining as part of their Dracula costumes. Although I couldn't see Brooks as a murderer, it was possible that his strong feelings for Monique could have led to a tragedy if they'd quarreled. Since I'd met Todd only once, I didn't really know him, but he'd seemed sincere about his desire to marry Monique. Both men appeared to mourn her death, but that didn't mean that one of them couldn't have caused her fall.

Valerie and Frank made the list of possible suspects because they'd both worn red berets. Frank had certainly irritated Valerie with his inappropriate attention to Monique and his equally inappropriate actions of ignoring his new wife in favor of fawning over the Road-runner's newest member. I'd known both artists since I'd first joined the Roadrunner, and everybody else who knew them had been as delighted as I had when they'd decided to marry. Was there trouble in paradise? Again, it was difficult for me to believe that either of them could be a killer; difficult, but not impossible, given Frank's behavior and Valerie's jealousy.

The mysterious woman dressed as Red Riding Hood certainly qualified as having the reddest costume I'd seen at the party, but I had no idea who she was, and neither did anyone else I'd asked.

Was the killer one of these five people or someone else?

Chapter 19

And what about Monique's missing phone? Lieutenant Belmont told me that the cops had searched the limo she'd taken to the party and come up with nothing. As I mulled over the mystery, it struck me that Monique hadn't gone straight from the Resort to Carrie's party. She'd told Brooks that she had to go to her dressmaker's house first to get her costume. Since Lonesome Valley was a small community, I figured that there were probably fewer than a handful of dressmakers in town.

I was about to lose the light anyway, so I cleaned my brush and put my paints away. Then, I searched on my laptop and found only one dressmaker listed. According to her basic, one-page website, she specialized in alterations, though, but she did list "custom clothing" as another service she offered. Knowing that she probably wouldn't give me any information about her customers, I called to inquire as to whether she'd be able to make me an evening gown, but she said she was doing alterations only now and no longer made custom clothing.

I decided to call Belle, who was a member of Lonesome Valley's sewing guild, to find out whether she knew of anyone else who might have made Monique's gown.

"Only one woman I know of—Nancy Keaton," Belle told me after I posed the question to her. "Nancy has so much business that she doesn't need to advertise."

"No wonder I couldn't find her on the web."

"She's a member of the sewing guild. That's how I met her, but she doesn't come to our meetings very often anymore, probably because she's so swamped. Nancy makes a lot of wedding gowns and bridesmaids' dresses."

"So she'd have been able to make Monique's costume?"

"No doubt. She can just look at a garment and copy it. But why do you ask?"

I explained that Monique's phone was missing and the reason the police were looking for it.

"Would you like me to call her? I'm sure she'd tell me if she's the one who made Monique's costume."

"That'd be great. Thanks, Belle."

"I'll do it right now."

Less than a minute later, Belle called me back.

"No luck getting her on the phone, but I can try later, maybe after dinner. She's probably busy right now, and I know she turns her phone off when she's working."

Emma and I had just finished clearing up after our own dinner when Belle came to the door.

"Still no luck contacting Nancy, but I'm sure that if we went over to her house, she'd answer the door. Want to give it a try?"

"Of course. That's a good idea. Let me grab my purse and change back into that sweater I was wearing earlier."

My daughter looked a bit surprised when I told her that Belle and I were off to see a dressmaker but wouldn't be gone too long. I didn't tarry long enough to explain our mission, although Emma could have hardly objected on the grounds that it would be dangerous to visit Nancy.

When we arrived at Nancy's house, several lights shone from the windows.

"Looks like she's home."

"Yes," Belle said as we exited her car. "I think she'll talk to us since we came over to see her, even though she's not answering her phone."

We climbed the few steps to the porch, and Belle rang the doorbell. We stood back and waited. It wasn't long until we heard footsteps and the door swung open.

"Belle! What a surprise! Come on in."

"I'd like you to meet my friend and next-door neighbor Amanda."

We exchanged pleasantries, and Nancy invited us to her den in the back of the house.

Belle and I sat on a sofa while Nancy perched on a chair. I could tell she wondered what we were doing there, but she was too polite to pose such a blunt question.

"I tried to call you earlier, but there was no answer. I know you're busy, but we just needed to ask you a question, and we'll be on our way."

"It's fine. I was about to knock off for the evening, anyway. I've just finished a bridal gown and six bridesmaids' dresses. The bridal party will be here tomorrow morning for their fittings, and I really had to hustle to get done in time."

"Sounds like business is booming."

"It's so busy that I can hardly keep up, but having a lot of business beats the alternative."

I nodded. Because I felt exactly the same, I could certainly understand Nancy's perspective.

"I'm running on, though. You said you had a question."

"Uh, yes. We were wondering whether Monique d'Albert might have left her phone here Saturday night."

"Monique? Why, no. As far as I know, she hasn't called me about it, but, of course, I haven't been answering my phone." Left unsaid, but obvious from Nancy's quizzical stare, was her confusion about why *we* would be asking.

"So you haven't heard about Monique?" I asked.

"Heard what?"

"She fell off a balcony at the party Saturday night. Unfortunately, she didn't survive the fall."

The shocked expression on Nancy's face confirmed that she hadn't heard the bad news.

"I can't believe it. That poor girl! She was so happy when she left here that evening. She loved her dress and couldn't wait to show it off. I seldom listen to the news, and, as you know, I don't answer the phone when I'm busy, either. Oh, this is terrible!"

"The police haven't been able to find her phone, and it occurred to me that maybe she could have left it here."

"The police? But, why?"

"Nancy, they don't think her fall was an accident," Belle explained gently. "Perhaps if they know who she was in contact with before the party, it might help."

"Oh, dear. I can't believe it," Nancy repeated. "I haven't noticed her phone, but we can look around for it." The dressmaker stood and led us into a large room that was arranged into three areas by the careful placement of folding room dividers and clothing racks. Behind the dividers was a dressing area; a couple of clothing racks stood in front of another area where a steam iron and a couple of sewing machines as well as a large table stood. When we came into the room, we were in the waiting area, which contained a long sofa, a couple of armchairs and a coffee table with the latest issues of wedding magazines.

"Monique sat here while she waited for me to bring her dress out," Nancy said, pointing to the plush sofa. "I don't remember seeing her phone, but now I remember that she took the clothes she'd been wearing when she came out to the limo in a large shopping bag. Maybe the phone ended up in the bag."

"Hmm. Lieutenant Belmont said they searched the limo that she took to the party, so they must have found that bag, or maybe the driver turned it in back at the Resort."

"Let's check the sofa, just in case," Belle suggested, "if it's OK with you, Nancy."

"Of course. It wouldn't be the first time one of my customers lost something between the cushions."

Belle started on one end of the sofa while I searched the other end. When we met in the middle and pulled the center cushion off the couch, we spotted a phone that had slipped down in back of the cushion.

"That has to be it," I said. "I'd better call Lieutenant Belmont."

"I'll set it on the coffee table," Nancy said, as she started to reach for the phone.

"Better leave it right there until the police come. We probably shouldn't touch it," I said.

"Oh, I get it. It could be evidence," Nancy said. "Maybe we should wait in the living room until they show up."

As we trooped back through the house to the living room in the front, I called Lieutenant Belmont.

"I think we found Monique's phone," I told him as soon as he answered.

"Where are you?"

I gave him Nancy's address and was rewarded with a groan. A second later the doorbell chimed.

"Answer the door, Nancy Drew. We're on the front porch."

I hurried to the front door and pulled it open. There on the porch stood the lieutenant, Dave Martinez, and Sergeant Boyd, and I realized they'd already been out front when I called.

"Trying to beat me to it, are you?"

"No. It just happened to occur to me that Monique could have forgotten her phone when she left her dressmaker's house for the party."

I stood aside and motioned for the three to step in. Meanwhile, Nancy and Belle came into the foyer. Lieutenant Belmont had pulled a small notebook from his pocket and was consulting it.

"You reported that the victim arrived for the party in a limo from the Resort. There's nothing mentioned about any stop-over," the lieutenant said pointedly as he glared at Sergeant Boyd. I assumed the unfortunate detective had either neglected to tell the lieutenant that Monique had changed into her costume for the party at Nancy's house or that he'd never uncovered that detail in his inquiries. If the latter, it was certainly a big oversight on the sergeant's part.

Embarrassed, Boyd mumbled, "Sorry, Lieutenant."

I had a feeling the hapless newcomer was going to be even sorrier when they returned to the police station.

"Show me the phone," the lieutenant demanded, ignoring both Nancy and Belle.

Despite the lieutenant's rudeness, Nancy politely said, "Come this way, sir."

We all followed her into her sewing studio, and she pointed to the sofa where the phone lay next to the cushion we'd pulled out when we were searching for it.

"It's right where we found it," I stated. "It must have slipped behind the cushion when Monique was sitting on the sofa, waiting for Nancy to bring her dress out."

"Dave," the lieutenant gestured toward the phone, and Dave whipped out his phone and snapped a few pictures of the phone where it lay before he gloved up and then produced an evidence bag and slipped the device inside.

"Boyd, don't you have an interview to conduct?" the lieutenant asked.

Like a deer in the headlights, Boyd froze. "Uh, yes, sir," he said, although he made no move to question Nancy.

"What's your name, ma'am?" Dave asked in an effort to head off more trouble as the lieutenant glowered at Boyd.

"Nancy Keaton."

"Sergeant Boyd needs to ask you a few questions. It shouldn't take long."

"All right." Nancy said, looking expectantly at Boyd.

"Let's get out of here," Lieutenant Belmont said to Dave before scowling at Boyd.

I didn't envy Lonesome Valley's newest police sergeant.

"You're not going to leave that young man here without a ride, are you, Bill?" Belle asked.

Sometimes I tended to forget that both Dennis and Belle knew the lieutenant although it wasn't a happy acquaintance since, years ago, the lieutenant had been kicked out of a photography club that both he and Dennis belonged to. Dennis was still a member, in fact.

"Don't be ridiculous. We'll be waiting for him in the car. How did *you* get involved in all this, anyway?"

Belle just shrugged and smiled sweetly.

"Never mind. I know you live next door to *her*. If you want to spend your time playing Dr. Watson to her Sherlock Holmes, I guess I can't stop you, but be careful. The killer might take notice."

The lieutenant opened the front door and walked out, but before Dave followed him, he turned to me and said, "See you Saturday."

I raised my eyebrows.

"For the kids' painted pumpkins event at the gallery. I promised Dawn that I'd help out."

Chapter 20

Dave's words had reminded me that I'd promised to bring a couple of painted pumpkins to the Saturday afternoon event at the Road-runner, where we'd be sharing ideas about different ways to paint the traditional Halloween decorations, so the following morning I set up two medium-size pumpkins on a table in my studio and rummaged through my supply closet in search of my acrylic paints.

Since oil paint was my preferred medium, I hardly used acrylics at all. Their tendency to dry very quickly was a big downside, as far as I was concerned. With oils, I had more time to blend the paint until I achieved just the right hue, and I firmly believed that they produced a depth of color that I'd never succeeded in matching with acrylics. Besides, some collectors definitely preferred oil paintings to acrylic paintings, and I thought using oils expanded my potential market, even if only marginally.

Finally, I located my box of acrylic paints in the back of the closet, behind an old easel. I decided to make the two pumpkins count double, with faces on each side, rather than just the one that a jack-o-lantern would have. Of course, these pumpkins wouldn't be carved. That was part of the fun of painting them—no messy removal of seeds would be necessary. I decided to avoid the traditional scary look that most jack-o-lanterns have and paint some cute whimsical faces. I wanted to keep them fairly easy so that the kids could paint similar ones if they liked. Five of us—Valerie, Frank, Susan, Chip, and I—would be displaying our examples and then circulating to answer any questions our attendees might have after a brief demo by Frank.

I made quick work of my project and ended up with a cute kitty and an adorable puppy on one pumpkin and a bat and a spider on the other. I was cleaning my brushes and appreciating the fact that acrylic paint cleaned up well with water, which I had to admit was much easier and less toxic than cleaning oil paint from my brushes with turpentine, when my phone rang. I set the brushes on a paper towel to dry and picked up.

"Amanda, I'm calling everybody to let them know that we've had a burglary at the gallery," Pamela said. "I was sure I'd locked up when I left yesterday, but the door was open when I got here this morning—not standing open, but unlocked."

"Oh, no! Was anything stolen?"

"I'm afraid so, and it's very strange. Every one of Monique's pastels is gone. They were in the back, so I didn't notice right away. I checked all around, including the apartment upstairs, and nothing else is missing. Of course, the police have been here, and Bill doesn't know what to make of it. It's almost as though someone's still targeting Monique. Do you think her killer could have taken the pastels?"

"You mean as a trophy or something?" I asked.

"I don't know. I guess that's kind of far out."

"Not necessarily. We don't know who we're dealing with. I'm starting to wonder if she had a stalker."

"How about that woman, the so-called detective, who came in looking for her?" Pamela asked.

"The police know who she is. Remember they talked to her a couple of times the night she scared the wits out of Monique. Surely Lieutenant Belmont will be looking into her whereabouts at the time that the gallery was robbed."

"Come to think of it, I forgot to mention her when the police were here, and Bill didn't say anything about it. He may not even know. The incident was handled by patrol officers. I think I'll give him a call. By the way, I just wanted everyone to know that I'm going to add some extra layers of security, and I'll be much more careful to make sure the door's locked when I leave. In fact, I'll have someone else verify it each time."

I wished the robbery hadn't happened, and not just because Monique's work was gone and all of the members would be concerned about whether or not their own artwork might become a target, but also because Pamela was already dealing with more than enough problems. At least, no vandalism to the gallery had occurred.

"You know, there are two other people who've expressed interest in what would happen with Monique's pastels in the last few days." I said.

"Faye and Monique's lawyer, you mean?"

"Right, but, on the other hand, Faye did agree to keep them hanging in the gallery until the end of the year, and Todd's gone along with leaving them at the Roadrunner for now, so it doesn't seem as though either of them would have any reason to take them."

"I doubt it." Pamela agreed. "I can't imagine Monique's own lawyer doing such a thing, and when I mentioned to Faye that the pastels could be sold for quite a sum, her eyes lit up for just a second. Then she looked away. It was after I told her their value that she said it would be all right to leave the pastels in the gallery. I think you were on the right track about the private detective, but what's her motive?"

"I don't know unless Edward McCall's daughter put her up to it. Maybe it's as simple as spite." I speculated. "Those pastels meant the world to Monique."

"Sounds crazy to me, but I know people do weird things sometimes."

"I remember how scared she was that night the PI was knocking on the gallery door. Monique left Palm Springs to come here, maybe to put some distance between her and her step-daughter."

"Her step-daughter who's thirty years older than Monique was," Pamela commented.

"Probably one of the reasons she hated Monique, along with the fact that she didn't want Monique to get her hands on McCall's money. I bet she was jealous, too. Not an ideal situation."

"No, it wasn't," Pamela agreed. "Well, I'd better go. I need to notify some more of the members about the break-in and call Bill to let him know about the private detective."

Since I'd finished my pumpkin painting right before Pamela had called me, it was time to get down to business and work on my latest oil painting. I should be able to accomplish a great deal as long as I stuck to my plan and spent the rest of the day and tomorrow painting. Other than spending a few minutes tidying the studio for tomorrow evening's weekly studio tour and taking some periodic breaks, I promised myself to stay on task. I was looking forward to some fun and a longer break on the weekend, and I hoped nothing would happen to interfere.

Just as I had that thought, my phone rang. With an unexpected feeling of foreboding, I answered.

"I have good news and bad news," Brian announced.

Chapter 21

"Better give me the bad news first," I said, holding my breath.

"Unfortunately, I won't be able to come home this weekend. All the site managers have been called to a mandatory meeting at headquarters. I leave tomorrow morning."

"All weekend, then?"

"That's the word. They told us to expect to be there at least until Sunday night, but it may run into Monday. I'm sorry, Amanda. I was looking forward to the weekend."

"Even the pet parade?" I teased.

"Well, seeing a bunch of dogs in Halloween costumes might not have been at the top of my list, but I certainly wanted to see *you*."

"I'll miss you, too. What about next weekend? Do you think you'll be able to make it?"

"Yep. I'll be there unless there's a major emergency. Like I said, there is some good news. The company directors booted our CEO and hired a new guy whose management style is fair and reasonable. I know because I've worked for him before. He's not a micro-manager, and he won't let anybody who works for him be one, either, so I'm looking forward to actually enjoying my job again, without having to jump at someone else's whim."

"Great! I'm so happy to hear it. I'm disappointed that you won't be here this weekend, but it's wonderful that your job will be like it used to be."

Brian's news surprised me, but I was quite relieved that he wouldn't be under the extreme pressure at work that he'd experienced over the past several months. Although I'd miss his company over the upcoming weekend, when we'd planned to spend most of our time together, I'd just have to make the best of the situation. After all, I had plenty to do to occupy myself with the pumpkin painting event at the gallery and the pet parade on Sunday.

When I returned to my latest creation, I thought that, even though I hadn't planned on working at all on Saturday or Sunday, I should do some painting then, too.

By the time Friday evening rolled around, I was ready for a break. Of course, I enjoyed painting. I would never have attempted to make my living as a painter if I felt ambivalent about my artwork, but I'd been hard at it every chance I'd had all week, and I welcomed the opportunity to relax a bit and talk about my artwork, rather than working on it, if anyone came by my open studio. There had been weeks when nobody showed up at all, but, thankfully, they were the exception, rather than the rule.

Since I'd waited until the last minute to finish tidying the studio, I hurriedly dusted and re-arranged a few items and moved the landscape I was currently painting to an easel behind my desk so that it wouldn't be accessible to the public. I didn't want an eager potential customer touching the wet paint. I'd noticed that visitors often reached out to feel the texture on one of my oil paintings, so I made sure to hang only those paintings that were dry on my studio walls. Early on, I'd made the mistake of leaving my easels with works in progress in place, and a child had smeared a frosted cookie all over one of my landscapes. After that, I made sure that any new works were out of reach, and I never served frosted cookies again.

Cheese, crackers, and wine, along with small bottles of spring water, comprised my refreshments now. After I set them out on a table near the studio door, I turned on the lights to illuminate the sidewalk to the separate studio entrance and wheeled my sign to the curb promptly at six o'clock.

Emma and Matt had already gone out for the evening, but I wouldn't be alone. As she frequently did during Friday night's open studio time, Belle would be keeping me company this evening. She arrived at my front door a few minutes after I'd finished my set-up. Although she never brought Mr. Big with her on these occasions because the little dog would have barked at anyone who came in, Laddie always seemed disappointed not to have his little buddy for companionship. Mr. Big's absence didn't stop Laddie from standing at the baby gate between the studio and living room and watching any visitors who might arrive. Most of them stopped to pet him, and he loved the attention. On more than one occasion, he'd proved such a distraction that my potential customers paid more attention to my dog than to my artwork, but I decided, if that were the case, they probably hadn't been serious buyers, anyway.

"Would you like some wine?" I asked Belle after Laddie settled down. "I just opened it."

"No, thanks, but I'd love a cup of decaf."

"Coming right up. I think I'll join you." I didn't usually drink much coffee in the evening, whether regular or decaf, but a nice cup of java sounded good at the moment.

After I made the coffee, Belle and I settled ourselves in the living room, with our mugs, while Laddie lay at my feet and Mona Lisa curled up on the end of the sofa, opposite Belle. As we chatted, Belle keep a watchful eye outside to alert me to anyone who parked out front.

After half an hour of so, my first visitor arrived.

"Looks like only one person is getting out of the car," Belle told me.

I stepped over the baby gate, into the studio. Since getting over the gate was quite an ungainly maneuver, I'd learned never to wear any kind of a skirt for Friday studio tours. This evening I'd dressed in dark-wash jeans and a green drapey top accented with one of my hand-dyed abstract silk scarves in green and plum hues.

"Welcome to my studio," I greeted my visitor.

Most likely about ten years older than me, with short salt-and-pepper hair and dressed in a conservative navy pantsuit, the woman smiled and responded, "I've been wanting to visit some of the artists' studios for a long time, but, somehow, I keep putting it on the back burner."

"Have we met before?" I asked. "You look familiar."

"Perhaps at the Ian Adams Gallery in Scottsdale? I've been to a couple of their show openings."

"That must be it!" I exclaimed. "I've been to only one myself, even though I'm represented by the gallery."

"How does gallery representation work, anyway? Can artists have their work in more than one gallery?"

"Oh, sure, but usually only one gallery per town or area, although the terms of the agreement can be subject to negotiation between the artist and the gallery owner. Most gallery owners want to be an artist's sole representation in a given city. I'm represented by the Roadrunner here, Ian Adams Gallery in Scottsdale, and Crystal Star Gallery in Kansas City. Actually, since each gallery has its own clientele, there's seldom any overlap as far as customers go."

"That makes sense. I suppose I have a lot to learn about the art world. I recognized your name when I was looking at the tour map and trying to decide which stops to make. I'm a newbie when it comes to collecting art, but a friend of mine gave me a small oil painting several months ago. I was intrigued enough to want more. Then, when I happened to encounter an artist at my work. . . . Never mind, I shouldn't have mentioned her."

"Who is she?" I asked, not able to restrain my curiosity at her odd comment. "Maybe I know her."

"I suppose you must have known her. I'm told she was a member of the Roadrunner."

"Oh, no," I murmured. "You must mean Monique. Do you work at the hospital?" I was fairly certain this woman wasn't a member of the Lonesome Valley Police Department.

"As a matter of fact, I do. I'm also the county coroner."

"Monique's death was a horrible tragedy. She looked so spectacular when she arrived last Saturday at the costume party in her beautiful pink dress and glitzy jewelry, and then the unthinkable happened. I'll never forget seeing her fall."

"Awful! And to think people seem to care more for what she had than for the lady herself."

"How so?"

"I've already had her cousin and her lawyer inquiring about when they could claim her personal belongings. The dress she wore was completely ruined; we had to cut her out of it. I doubt that they'd want that—it's beyond repair. And her jewelry—it's pretty stuff, but it's strictly new rhinestone costume."

"I think she probably bought it to wear to the party," I speculated.

"Her lawyer wanted an inventory of the items, which my assistant will provide as soon as he gets his paperwork to us, but, frankly, I'd think he'd be more concerned with the bulk of her estate. Didn't she recently inherit millions from her husband's estate?"

"Evidently not. Todd Whitman admitted that Monique's claim on Edward McCall's estate wasn't valid."

"I didn't realize that. Of course, it wouldn't do the poor woman any good, even if it were valid. Well, I've said way more than I should have, but I guess there's no harm done. Anyway, enough about my business; let's talk about yours."

Laddie panted in excitement as my visitor strolled toward one of my smaller landscapes that hung near the door. He thrust his head over the gate, and she stopped to pet him before looking at the painting.

"The view from Miners' Lookout?"

"That's right! Done in my style, a lot of people wouldn't have recognized it. I don't go in for realism in my landscapes."

"It's beautiful, and I love the colors." She stood back and gazed at the painting. "It's calling me; that's for sure. Let me look around a bit, but I have a feeling I'll be taking that one home with me."

The coroner, who'd never told me her name, took her time examining the other paintings on display. I noticed she gravitated toward the smaller pictures, and I wondered if she had in mind to hang the painting she chose in a particular spot in her home. She confirmed my supposition when she finally decided to purchase the Miners' Point landscape, telling me that it would look perfect over the console in her foyer.

She didn't blink twice at the price, as she pulled her credit card out of her wallet. I glanced at the name on the card—Allison Boyd—as she tapped it against my card reader. Briefly, I wondered whether she was related to Sergeant Boyd, but, as I put the painting into a box for her so that it would be protected, she asked me about framing options. When I suggested Brooks' frame shop at the Resort, she seemed happy that she wouldn't have to go to Phoenix for first-class framing, and she was out the door before I had a chance to ask her.

Chapter 22

"Great sale!" Belle said, when I returned to the living room.

"It certainly was. Even though occasionally nobody stops by, sales like tonight's remind me it's definitely worth it to be on the Friday night open studio tour."

"Sure is."

"I'm surprised the coroner talked about Monique's case, aren't you?"

"Yes; it was kind of ironic that she kept talking, even though she said a couple of times that she shouldn't."

"I know; that was strange, but we did learn something. Both Faye and Todd asked about Monique's personal belongings."

"What do you make of it?"

"Maybe something; maybe nothing. I guess they've both been involved in making final arrangements—I hear Monique's memorial service will be Monday—and taking care of everything else that needs to be done. Todd's the executor of Monique's estate, so I suppose he has to round up all the information. On the other hand, he's one of the guests who was wearing red at the party, so he's a potential suspect. I can't really see what his motive would be, though. Without any claim on McCall's estate, Monique didn't have much money, so controlling her assets can't be a motive. Plus, Todd claims to have been in love with Monique; he wanted to marry her."

"A lovers' quarrel gone bad?"

"Always a possibility, I suppose. As for Faye, she wasn't even at the party as far as I know. At one point, I did wonder whether she could have been the woman in the Red Riding Hood costume. She's the right height, but her voice sounds different. Red Riding Hood had kind of a husky voice, but Faye's is more high-pitched. Of course, she could have been there in a different costume, but she wasn't on the guest list. Granted, she was angry with her cousin last week when she flirted with her husband, but now she seems genuinely upset at Monique's death."

"Like you said, their inquiries may mean nothing."

"There's really not much to go on. I wonder if the police found out anything from Monique's phone records or the phone itself. Of course, Lieutenant Belmont wouldn't ever tell me if they had revealed some clues."

"No, he wouldn't," Belle agreed. "The wonder is that you actually get along with him, sort of. Dennis never has been able to stand the guy, and Bill knows it, so I'm persona non grata, too, as far as he's concerned because I'm married to Dennis."

"I could tell from the way he ignored you when we saw him at Nancy's house. He didn't make any effort to be polite, but then he seldom does, with one exception. He treats Pamela very differently from everyone else. I'm beginning to think he likes her."

"You mean *like* likes her?"

"I do. She doesn't see it. She thinks he's just being kind, but she ought to have heard enough about him from Susan and me—Chip, too, for that matter—to know better."

"Well, how about that? I can't remember Bill ever having a girl-friend in the time we've known him. He's such a curmudgeon. But maybe he wasn't always a big grump."

"It's hard for me to think of him any other way."

We laughed and turned our conversation to our plans for the week-end. Since Emma was scheduled to work all day Saturday, Laddie would be spending the afternoon with Belle and Mr. Big while I helped out at the Roadrunner's pumpkin painting event. Then, on Sunday afternoon, we'd dress up the dogs in their Halloween costumes and attend the pet parade. When Dennis had found out that Brian wouldn't be able to come with us to the pet parade, he'd bailed, too, so Belle and I would be on our own with our cute canines. Belle and I were looking forward to it, but I was fairly sure that Dennis and Brian thought we were a bit silly to be dressing up our dogs for the upcoming holiday. Anyway, I told myself that it was fun to act frivolous sometimes.

Over an hour passed, and I was beginning to wonder whether the coroner would be the only person who came to my open studio when a couple in their thirties arrived and spent quite a while browsing while they helped themselves to the cheese, crackers, and wine. After looking through all my prints and hand-dyed silk scarves while her husband took photos of my paintings, the woman purchased a small box of note cards and they were on their way.

"You had to work pretty hard for that sale," Belle said.

"Yes, I was starting to think they might just camp out for the night in my studio. I think it was a net loss, though. The wine cost me more than the note cards cost them. That's the way it goes, though. At least, they bought something; most people don't."

"I noticed the guy took a lot of pictures. I haven't ever seen anybody do that here before."

"They usually don't. I know some artists and galleries don't allow it, but I figure my artwork is already accessible to the public, whether it's on my website or in a gallery, so if someone's intent on stealing an image, they'll probably find a way. A lot of times when someone's considering a purchase, they'll take a picture to get a second opinion, so it can be a good thing. I have a feeling our photographer was killing time tonight while his wife looked around. They may have been my last customers of the evening."

"I don't think so," Belle said, as she turned to peek out the window. "A pickup truck just parked out front. Looks like a woman and a little girl."

I stepped back over the baby gate, ready to greet the pair when they entered the studio. Swishing his tail back and forth, Laddie stood at the gate in eager anticipation.

"Welcome to my studio," I said as soon as the mother and daughter crossed the threshold.

"Hello, I'm Rhonda Whelan, and this is my daughter Serena."

"Nice to meet you. I'm Amanda Trent. Feel free to have a look around and let me know if you have any questions."

"Thanks, Amanda. I thought I'd bring Serena to see what a real artist's studio looks like. She's signed up for the pumpkin painting class at the Roadrunner tomorrow."

"Hi, Serena," I said, but the little girl, who was probably around seven or eight years old had eyes only for my canine companion. "Would you like to pet Laddie? He's very friendly."

"Can I, Mom?"

"Sure, go ahead," she said, and her daughter immediately went to Laddie and began to stroke his soft fur. Turning to me, she commented, "He looks like a golden retriever."

"Yes, he's my golden boy. He's such a good dog, very sweet."

"I wish we had a dog," the little girl said softly.

"Maybe some day when we get a house. You know we're not allowed to have pets in the apartment."

Seeing the sad look on Serena's face, I decided to try to distract her. "Would you like to see a couple of pumpkins I painted? You'll see them and lots more at the Roadrunner tomorrow, but you can have a sneak peek now."

Serena nodded solemnly, and I took the pumpkins out of my storage closet and set them on my desk so that Serena could get a closer look.

"How cute!" her mother exclaimed. "You're going to paint your own pumpkin tomorrow."

Serena looked as though she wasn't too sure that painting a pumpkin would be much fun. I had a feeling her attendance at the event had been her mother's idea, not Serena's.

"Do I have to make mine like these? I don't like spiders or bats," she complained, "and I'm no good at drawing, so I can't make faces."

"You can make yours any way you want," I assured her. "If you want a pumpkin that looks like a jack-o-lantern, we can show you how to use stencils. You don't have to draw or paint freehand if you don't want to."

"OK," she murmured reluctantly.

"Serena, it'll be fun," her mother nudged her. "You might make some new friends while you're at the gallery, too."

"I don't want new friends. I want my old friends. I want to go home," Serena wailed.

"Hush, honey. You know we can't do that. I have to start my new job Monday." She glanced at me. "Sorry, we just moved here. I know it'll take a while to adjust to the change. We came from Kansas City."

"No kidding; what a coincidence! I moved here from Kansas City myself, coming up on two years ago, and I love it here. I hope you and Serena will, too."

"So do I. My new job will be a big improvement over my old one, but it's tough to move and leave friends behind, especially for Serena. We hated to uproot her, but, financially, moving here to take a better job was pretty much a necessity if we ever wanted to accumulate enough money for a down payment on a house."

"I understand, and it takes time to get used to a new place. I'll keep a special eye on Serena tomorrow, make sure she meets some other kids, and help her with her project, if she likes."

"Thank you *so* much! I really appreciate it. Did you hear that, Serena?"

"Un, huh," Serena said, looking at her shoes.

"We'd better get going now. See you tomorrow, Amanda."

Chapter 23

I did indeed see Serena and her mother the next day when I arrived at the gallery an hour before the pumpkin painting event was scheduled to begin. Considering that Serena hadn't exactly seemed thrilled about participating, I was a bit surprised that she hadn't backed out, but perhaps Rhonda had insisted that her daughter attend. There was just one problem, though. They were an hour early.

"Hi, Amanda," Rhonda said, as she approached the door with Serena in tow.

"Glad you could make it," I replied. "We'll be starting at two."

"Oh, no! I must have mixed up the time." She turned to her daughter and said, "Let's go join Daddy at the bookstore, Serena."

"Do we *have* to? Daddy never wants to leave."

"You know books are Daddy's business," she told her daughter. Rhonda looked at me and explained, "My husband's a freelance book editor. It's lucky he works remotely from home, or I might not have been able to accept my promotion."

"I love working at home myself. It has its advantages. Anyway, there are plenty of other shops to browse here along Main Street if you don't want to spend an hour at the bookstore. Maybe Serena would enjoy some of them. I'd better go inside now; we need to get everything set up. Pumpkin painting will be in our meeting room, so just come on back when you get here."

As I opened the door to the gallery, I could hear Serena begging her mother to stop at the candy store a few doors down from the Roadrunner, but I went inside before I could hear Rhonda's reply.

Pamela and Ralph greeted me when I came in and told me that Chip and Susan had already delivered the pumpkins to the meeting room, but Valerie and Frank hadn't arrived yet, nor had Dawn and Dave.

"I'm sure they'll be here soon," Pamela said. "I put some of the supplies out, but I'm not sure what else Frank and Valerie wanted. They've pretty much run our children's art classes by themselves for the last couple years. I'm sure they'll appreciate having so much help this time."

"I don't know how much help I'll be, since I have no teaching experience, but I'll do my best."

"Don't worry; Frank will take care of the demo, and then everyone can circulate and help the kids who get stuck or have questions."

"Better you than me, Amanda," Ralph commented. "Give me adult students any day of the week." Although Ralph winked, I wasn't sure whether he was kidding or not. Maybe not, since I knew all the classes he'd ever taught were for adults.

"You're just in time," Susan said when I walked into the meeting room. "We're going to put a basic palette of acrylic paint on these plastic plates and set one at every place."

"Hey, Amanda," Chip greeted me. "I'll get the brushes, cups of water, and a cloth for everyone, too, and then we can have all this stuff set up and ready to go when the kids get here."

The long tables in the meeting room were already covered with plastic tablecloths, and one pumpkin had been set at each place. A table in the back of the room held more pumpkins.

Susan saw me glance at the pumpkins. "We have enough for everyone to paint two pumpkins. There are some extras. I guess we can raffle them off maybe, if any of the kids want more than two."

"Sounds good."

While Susan and I squeezed blobs of acrylic paint from large tubes onto the plastic plates, Chip got busy putting the other items next to the pumpkins on the tables. Twenty children had pre-registered. Pamela had made it clear that we didn't have the space for more, so registration had been a necessity, and we didn't expect any walk-ins.

The door to the meeting room was open, so it was no surprise that we could hear conversations that took place outside the room in the hallway. As Susan and I finished placing the acrylic paint palettes at each place, we heard Valerie urging Frank to hurry up.

"I'm coming," he said irritably. "Don't get on your high horse again."

"*Me*? You should talk," Valerie replied.

"Uh, oh," Susan said. "I hope they calm down before our class starts."

"So do I. Otherwise, things could get pretty awkward."

Although his wife had been the one who'd wanted to hurry, Frank entered the room alone.

"Valerie will be here in a minute," he said. "She had to stop to powder her nose." He held up two fingers on each hand and wiggled them up and down to mimic quotes when he said "powder her nose."

"We've set up a place for each student," Chip told him.

Frank glanced at the tables and nodded. He walked to the back of the room and grabbed a couple of pumpkins.

"For my demo," he said.

"I thought you were going to bring a couple of painted pumpkins, too." Susan said. "We each brought a couple." She pointed to a side table where we'd set our finished pumpkins.

"I decided to wing it. I'll demo a couple of faces, and you all can talk about how you painted yours, but keep it short, so the kids will have plenty of time to paint their own. There are five of us, so they can have plenty of individual help, if they need it. I called Dawn to let her know we wouldn't need her and Dave, so they won't be coming."

Red-eyed, Valerie slipped into the room while Frank was talking. She hadn't brought any pumpkins with her, either.

"Do you want me to do a demo, too?" she asked her husband.

"That won't be necessary," he snapped. "I've got it covered."

Frank fiddled around gathering tubes of paint and other supplies, which he placed on the front table, next to the pumpkins, for his demo. The rest of us didn't say a word. If his bad mood persisted, the painting lesson wouldn't be much fun for the kids.

"Where are the stencils?" Frank demanded suddenly.

Chip shrugged. "How would we know, man? You're in charge of the kids' classes."

"Sorry, Chip. *We* should have been more organized," he stated, looking to throw the blame on Valerie.

"They're in the storage cabinet in the upstairs studio," Valerie told us, giving Frank an icy stare. "I think the cabinet's locked. Pamela keeps the keys in her office, but I should have mine here somewhere.

She opened her purse and came up with a key, tagged "RR-upstairs storage cabinet."

I reached for it. "I'll get the stencils," I said, eager to leave the feuding couple behind for a few minutes. I was beginning to wish I'd never volunteered to help.

"Why don't you let me do it, Amanda?" Chip asked. I figured he was probably just as anxious to take a break from the tension as I was.

"It's fine; I won't be a minute."

"I'll help," Chip insisted, as he followed me out the door and up the steps to the second floor, where we found the studio door locked.

Since Chip used the studio himself, he had his own key, so I waited while he searched his pockets for it, coming up empty.

"Sorry, I must have left it at home," he apologized.

"That's OK. I'll just run downstairs and get Pamela's."

I hurried back downstairs, almost running into Pamela as I reached the first floor.

"Oops, sorry, Pamela. I'm looking for the key for the upstairs studio. Fred wants to have stencils available for the students, and I guess they're stored in the cabinet up there."

"Here you go," Pamela said, reaching into her pocket and producing several keys all attached to a key ring. She held the entire ring up by one of the keys, telling me, "This one is for the studio."

"Thanks," I said, a bit out of breath as I took it from her. "I'll bring it right back."

Despite my breathlessness, I ran up the stairs, only to find that the door to the studio was open. When I went inside, I found Chip standing in front of the open cabinet with his hand on a distinctive picture frame sitting on a shelf inside.

Immediately, I recognized the frame. There was only one Road-runner artist whose artwork was all framed in elaborate and pricey gilt frames.

Chip had his hand on one of Monique's missing pastels.

Chapter 24

I gasped. Chip's caught-with-his-hand-in-the-cookie-jar expression told the story. I rushed inside and closed the door behind me. As I came closer to the open cabinet, I could see that it was full of Monique's artwork.

"*You*?" I asked in astonishment.

"No, I. . . I was just looking for the stencils."

"Chip, I can tell you're fibbing. What's going on?"

"Oh, all right. I thought I could grab the stencils before you got back with the key to the door."

"Which you had all along, and you obviously had your own key to the cabinet, too."

He nodded. "Look, Amanda, I was only doing what Monique asked me to do. At least, I think that's what she wanted."

"What in the world are you talking about?"

"The night she died, remember?"

"I'm not likely to forget."

"Me, either. It was horrible. What I meant was: do you remember when she was whispering to me?"

"Yes. You never mentioned what she said to you. I figured she was asking for help and you were trying to comfort her."

"That's right, and then she begged me to take her pastels to protect them."

I frowned. "Odd. Can you remember her exact words?"

"She said, 'My pastels; save my pastels.' Then she opened her eyes and looked straight into mine. That's when she said, 'Please, Chip, don't let them be destroyed.' And I promised her I wouldn't. I don't know why she was worried about her artwork, but it was her dying wish that I save it."

I stared at the open cabinet and rubbed my forehead. "Chip, you have to tell Pamela. I understand why you did what you did, but you know Pamela thought there'd been a robbery, and now the police are involved."

"But there's no crime. I didn't remove Monique's pastels from the gallery. They're still here. I didn't break in, either. I used my key."

"I don't know why Monique thought her pastels were in danger, but you can't go on with this. Because of what you've done, Pamela made a false report to the police. Not only that, but you let her think *she* forgot to lock the gallery door."

"I know. I feel bad about that, but I made sure the gallery was safe. After I left, I watched from the Coffee Klatsch to make sure that nobody tried the front door. After about half an hour, Pamela showed up to open the gallery."

"You know what you have to do. Those pastels need to go right back on the wall downstairs, and you have to tell Pamela. Lieutenant Belmont's going to be livid when he hears about this."

"Oh, I have a feeling he's likely to give Pamela a pass. After all, she really thought there was a robbery."

"He may well give *her* a pass, but, as for you. . . ."

Our conversation was interrupted by the rattling of the studio's door handle. I hadn't realized it, but the door had locked automatically when I'd closed it behind me.

"Hey, are you in there?" Susan called.

I hastened to the door and let her in.

"What's taking so long? Frank's getting more irritable by the minute. He said we need those stencils pronto. Chip, can't you find them?"

Since I'd been standing in front of her when she'd entered the room, I'd blocked Susan's view of the storage cabinet, but as soon as I stepped back, she could see the missing artwork inside.

She put her hand over her mouth and looked questioningly at her nephew.

"I can explain," he told her.

"This better be good," she muttered, "but save it for later. Kids are starting to arrive, and we need to be ready."

Chip reached up to the top shelf and brought down a large box. "Here. These are all the stencils. I'll be back downstairs in a minute. I need to make sure everything's locked up."

Susan grabbed the box, and I followed as she stalked out of the room.

"Unbelievable!" she muttered as we went downstairs, only to find our way blocked by someone wearing a navy blue hoodie coming up the stairs.

At first, the woman, who had her head down, tried to sidle by us.

"Excuse me," Susan said loudly. "Only Roadrunner members are allowed upstairs."

"I was looking for the restroom," the woman said, her eyes on the steps, rather than on Susan.

As soon as she spoke, I realized who she was.

"I don't think so," I said. "You were warned not to come into the gallery again. If we have to, we'll get a restraining order to keep you away."

She held up her hands in a gesture of surrender. "OK, OK, I'm going." She turned and went back downstairs, her motorcycle boots clattering all the way.

"I didn't recognize her at first," Susan told me. "She's that PI who scared Monique so much."

"I didn't, either, not until she spoke, and her husky voice gave her away. She smokes a lot, I think. That's probably why her voice sounds so raspy. And I just realized something else. She was at Carrie's party wearing a costume and a mask."

Susan stared at me.

"Red Riding Hood," I revealed, "and a prime suspect."

"You're going to tell Lieutenant Belmont, aren't you?" Susan asked. "I sure don't want to talk to him."

"No worries. I don't mind telling him about her crashing the party in a red costume and her skulking around the Roadrunner." We were downstairs now and saw that quite a crowd had gathered in the gallery. No wonder Pamela hadn't spotted the detective when she'd come in.

"What about the pastels? Are you going to tell Lieutenant Belmont where they are?"

"I'm sure Pamela will fill him in, after Chip tells her about it."

"Well, I wish somebody would fill *me* in," Susan said in exasperation, "but we really have to get back to the meeting room now. I hope Frank settles down before class starts."

"Me, too. We want the kids to enjoy painting their pumpkins. Nobody's going to enjoy anything if he keeps it up."

When we came into the meeting room, Frank greeted us with "at last" and grabbed the box out of Susan's hands.

That didn't go over very well with my friend.

"I've had about enough of your bad mood, Frank," Susan said in a low voice so that the students who'd already found a place to sit couldn't hear her. "You may be a board member, but so are Chip and Valerie, and so am I. We're going to have to ask you to leave if you can't conduct yourself in a professional manner."

Taken aback by Susan's blunt threat, Frank had the decency to look embarrassed.

"Uh, sorry, Susan. I'll shape up."

"You'd better because I meant every word."

I'd never witnessed Susan telling someone off before, but she'd certainly been effective this time because Frank immediately went around the room, cheerfully greeting each student who was already there, then went to the door and, with a big smile, welcomed the others as they came in.

"I guess you told him," I whispered.

"Good thing it worked," she whispered back. "I don't know whether Chip and Valerie would have gone along with throwing him out or not. Besides that, neither one of them is even in the room right now."

When Valerie returned a few minutes later, Frank pulled her aside and they spoke in low voices until Valerie nodded her head. They ended their confab with a quick kiss, so we figured that the couple had agreed to settle their argument.

Valerie went to the back of the room, picked up a pumpkin, and set it on the same table where Frank had put his supplies and pumpkin. It looked as though Valerie might be going to do a demo, too.

About half the students had checked in when Serena appeared with both her parents. Like Serena and her mother, Serena's father had dark hair and eyes, although his seemed a bit distorted behind glasses with thick lenses. He looked like my idea of a bookworm, so it was a bit ironic that, as an editor, he really did work with books all day. Rhonda introduced us, and then she looked around the room.

"Serena, isn't that Ava over there?"

About the same time Rhonda spoke, a little girl began motioning to Serena.

"I think she wants you to sit next to her," Rhonda said to Serena. "Let's go see."

I followed mother and daughter to make sure that Serena was settled. As it turned out, Ava was in Serena's class, and she invited Serena to sit next to her, so I was happy the newcomer had found a friend.

"Serena started school here three days ago. Ava's mother was the one who told me about this class, and I was lucky to get the last slot for Serena." Rhona told me.

"I'm glad she has a friend here. I'm sure they'll have fun."

"We'll be next door at the Coffee Klatsch or at the bookstore if you need us."

"Thanks for letting me know, but don't worry. I'm sure everything will be fine."

Serena and Ava were so busy giggling that Serena barely acknowledged her parents' departure, but as soon as Frank started the class with his demonstration about how to paint a ghostly face on his pumpkin, both girls stopped talking and watched what he was doing, as did the rest of the class. I'd been afraid that some of the kids might act rowdy, but they all paid attention as Frank showed them various painting techniques.

When Frank finished the spooky face, he flipped the pumpkin around and showed everyone how to make a cat's face with just a few paint strokes. Then he turned it over to Valerie, who used stencils to make faces that looked like a traditional jack-o-lantern. Chip, Susan, and I rounded out the program by showing our pumpkins and explaining that the students could paint a pumpkin with a Halloween theme, but they could pick another subject if they wanted to, and we each showed them what we'd done.

A few of the students started to paint immediately, but several others looked as though they couldn't quite decide what to do. I was keeping a close watch on Serena, and I could tell she was one of them, although her friend Ava was already busily painting flowers on her pumpkin.

"Serena, what would you like to paint?" I asked, remembering how she'd protested that she couldn't draw when she'd visited my studio the previous evening.

"Maybe something like that," she said, pointing to Valerie's jack-o-lantern face.

"Do you want to use stencils to help with the eyes?" I asked.

"Uh, huh, and the nose. Can I get a triangle stencil for the nose?"

"Sure. Let's go find what you need." We went to the table where all the supplies were, but just as Serena reached for a sheet of circle stencils, a little boy snatched it. Serena looked as though she might be on the verge of tears, but I quickly distracted her.

"Look, Serena," I said, finding another sheet of circles, "this is just what you need. Now let's find the triangles." I sorted through the pile and soon found what I was searching for. "Here you go."

"Is there one for the mouth?"

"No, but I'll show you how to make a mouth using those triangle stencils, OK?"

Returning to her place next to Ava, Serena sat down, and I showed her how to hold the stencil with her left hand while painting with her right hand.

"You can tape the stencil to the pumpkin if you don't want to hold it," I said, noticing that she seemed hesitant.

"OK," she said, and I grabbed some masking tape from the supply table and helped her line up the stencil. She worked slowly and care-fully and when the first eye she painted looked good, she waved me off.

In the meantime, Ava had a veritable garden on her very colorful pumpkin, and she was busy adding bees and lady bugs to the mix.

As I glanced around, I saw that a couple of the students had already completed painting one pumpkin and were starting on number two while others were just getting started. I saw lots of monstrous faces, many cute ones, and a bunch of witches, ghosts, bats, spiders, and black cats. Ava was one of only a few students who had gone the non-Halloween route and picked a different subject.

"Everything seems to be going well," Susan whispered to me. "Lucky that Frank and Valerie made up, just in the nick of time."

"Luck had nothing to do with it. If you hadn't gotten stern with Frank, they'd probably still be feuding. We have you to thank."

"It was a little stressful, but in all my years at the Roadrunner, I've never seen a member act like that right before a class, and I sure didn't want the students to be forced to endure Frank's bad mood."

"Well, I think we can relax on that score."

"Now, how about letting me in on what's going on with Chip and those pastels. He's already told me he's going to have to leave early to go to work. I know they're shorthanded at the pizza parlor, but it gives him a perfect excuse not to talk to me."

"I'll fill you in as soon as class is over. I'd better call Lieutenant Belmont then, too, and let him know about the private investigator hanging around."

"Call now, if you like. We have things pretty well in hand."

"I'd better wait until after class. I promised Serena's mom I'd keep an eye on her."

"OK. Oops, it looks as though someone needs a little help." Susan motioned to one of the younger boys who'd accidentally tipped over his water and was frantically trying to mop it up with a soggy paper towel.

After Susan picked up an entire roll of towels and went to his rescue, things went smoothly for the rest of the class. Frank borrowed students' cameras and took their pictures along with their painted pumpkins so that they wouldn't have to try to take selfies, and many of them were texting their pictures to friends and family members as the class wrapped up.

When Serena's parents came to pick her up, she proudly displayed her painted jack-o-lantern face on one pumpkin and a black cat she'd stenciled on another.

Chip had left for work before the class ended, so Frank, Valerie, Susan, and I made quick work of the clean-up before Frank and Valerie departed arm in arm.

While I called Lieutenant Belmont, Susan made a last sweep of the room to make sure everything was back in place.

I had to leave a message with Sergeant Boyd, though, since the lieutenant wasn't available.

Susan and I had just sat down at one of the tables so that I could let her know what Chip had told me about Monique's pastels when we saw a shadowy figure going by outside the meeting room's open door.

"Look who's back," I said.

Chapter 25

By the time Susan and I reached the hallway, the PI had vanished. We looked around the gallery and upstairs, but she was nowhere to be found. Annoyed that I hadn't been able to get through to Lieutenant Belmont earlier, I tried again with the same results.

Something had to be done about the interloper, although I knew it would probably be up to our Roadrunner members to keep a closer watch.

"I noticed the students seemed happy with their projects," Pamela commented, as we came back downstairs after searching the second floor.

"Yes, it went well," Susan told her, "but we have a problem. I don't think you noticed her because it's been so busy in the gallery this afternoon, but that PI was here."

"Oh, no! I thought we made it clear she wasn't welcome."

"We saw her twice, Pamela," I added. "The first time we asked her to leave, and she did. Then just a few minutes ago, we saw her sneaking down the hall. She's gone again now, but I did warn her that we might have to take out a restraining order if she shows up again. I even tried to call Lieutenant Belmont to let him know that, not only are we having a problem with her, but I also just realized that she was at

Carrie's party, wearing a Red Riding Hood costume and mask, so she certainly should be considered a suspect in Monique's death. Why she's still hanging around here is a mystery. Could be she's looking for something."

"I wonder if it could have anything to do with Monique's pastels," Pamela said.

Susan and I glanced at each other before Susan shrugged. "Even though she's a private detective, her behavior's strange; that's for sure."

I wanted to tell Pamela about Chip's hiding Monique's artwork, and I knew that Susan did, too, but we'd let him know it was up to him to confess what he'd done. Although he'd agreed to tell Pamela why he'd secreted Monique's pastels and that they'd never left the building, he was in no hurry to do so. As he left for work earlier, I'd heard Susan advising him that, if he didn't tell Pamela what he'd done by tomorrow, she was going to do it for him, even though, at the time, Susan didn't know why Chip had removed the pastels from the gallery wall.

"I may see Bill tonight," Pamela said. "If so, I'll tell him all about the PI."

Susan and I exchanged another furtive glance. Still, I figured the news was better coming from Pamela than from me. It didn't make me sad to find out I might be able to avoid talking to the lieutenant about the private detective.

"He can call me if he likes," I volunteered, "but, really, the only information I have about the PI's appearance at Carrie's party is that I briefly ran into her downstairs there, but I didn't realize who she was at the time because she was dressed in a Red Riding Hood costume and she was wearing a mask. It wasn't until she showed up here and

I heard her raspy voice again that I made the connection. It's not much to go on, but the fact that she was wearing red—her whole costume was red—and the fact that she wasn't an invited guest both seem suspicious."

"Do you really think she could be the killer?" Pamela asked.

"It's possible. She and Monique could have argued," I speculated. "We know Monique was scared of her."

"She really was," Susan confirmed. "That's why she moved to the Resort."

"Well, one reason, anyway," I said.

"What do you mean?" Pamela asked.

"If I don't miss my guess, Brooks was in line to be her next husband. She wasn't going to inherit anything from McCall, and she was used to a luxurious life style, which Brooks could certainly have provided for her, and he could have helped her art career with shows in his gallery, too. After all, they came close to being engaged once, and it's obvious to me that he still cared for her."

"I wonder if she felt the same," Susan said, "but, of course, we'll never know. After his experience with that gold-digger he married before, it seems to me he should have thought twice, especially since Monique left him for McCall."

"We never really do know about couples, do we? I thought I had a good marriage, and I was totally blindsided when my husband announced he was going to divorce me."

Susan and Pamela both jumped in to comfort me.

"Oh, don't get me wrong. I'm fine now although it was a bit rocky going there for a while. I'm actually thrilled with my new life here in Lonesome Valley. I just meant it's difficult to see into other peoples' lives. Take Valerie and Frank, for example. They seemed like the perfect match, but they've had their issues."

"So soon after they were married, too," Susan commented.

Our unspoken consensus was that, if Monique hadn't appeared out of the blue the previous week, Valerie and Frank would most likely still be acting like honeymooners.

It was a little before five by the time Susan and I left the gallery, and I headed home to a quiet evening spent with Laddie and Mona Lisa since Emma and Matt had a date. I was relieved that Lieutenant Belmont never called me, although I was sure Pamela had told him about our sighting of the private investigator at the gallery by then.

"Are you ready to roar tomorrow?" I asked Laddie as I got ready to turn in for the night. "You're going to be a lion, you know."

Chapter 26

He snuggled up to me, wagging his tail enthusiastically as if to say he was looking forward to wearing his costume in the pet parade. I stroked his soft fur and gave him a good-night pat as I thought about what a good boy he was. He'd have fun walking in the parade with Mr. Big and all the other dogs, and he'd love meeting new people at the nursing home, which I thought would be a stop along our way as we circled the block where the veterinary clinic was located.

Although we'd have a nice walk in the afternoon, we didn't skip our usual morning walk, after which I quietly went into the studio and painted for a couple of hours since Emma was still sleeping, and I didn't want to wake her. When she finally did wake up, we had a light breakfast of toast and fruit before she got ready to go to work while I finished a few chores around the house. I was glad I'd gotten in some painting, although I hadn't really planned to work on the weekend, because I'd be taking some time off Monday afternoon to attend the memorial service for Monique.

When my phone pinged with a new text, just as I finished loading the clothes dryer, I picked it up eagerly, hoping that the message was from Brian. He'd phoned while I was at the pumpkin painting class, and I'd missed his call. When I'd tried to reach him later, my call had gone straight to voicemail, so we never had connected, although he'd sent me a brief text sometime during the night to let me know that everything was fine.

As I picked up my phone, I saw that the new message was from Pamela, not Brian. In a rather terse message that she'd sent to all the members of the Roadrunner, she'd explained that there hadn't been a burglary at the gallery and that a member had "mistakenly" moved Monique's artwork, but that it was now back in place. She concluded by saying that, although no crime had taken place, she was going ahead with enhanced security measures, including surveillance cameras, both inside and outside the Roadrunner, because of "unauthorized" visits to the gallery. I knew immediately that she was referring to the private investigator who'd been snooping around.

Obviously, Chip had told Pamela that he'd hidden Monique's pastels upstairs in the gallery, and I knew that had to have been an uncomfortable conversation. Although I could understand Chip's reasons for removing Monique's artwork from the wall where it usually hung, I thought his actions had been impulsive, especially considering that he didn't really understand what Monique was trying to tell him. In any case, he simply wasn't authorized to take charge of her artwork, even if that's what she'd been asking him to do. Only her executor had that responsibility.

Since Pamela's text didn't call for a reply, I set my phone down on the kitchen counter, attached its cord, and plugged it in so that it would be fully charged when Belle and I took Mr. Big and Laddie to the pet parade.

Matt had picked up Emma for work, so I'd have my SUV available to drive us to the pet parade. After I took the towels out of the dryer, folded them, and put them away, I briefly considered wearing my Victorian bathing costume to the pet parade because I knew that some of the pet parents planned to dress in costume, but since Belle wasn't going to do that and it would be quite cool to wear it anyway, with the daytime high temperature predicted to be around fifty, I decided jeans, tennis shoes, and a warm jacket were a better option. After I changed, I called Belle and invited her to have a quick lunch at my house before leaving for the vet clinic, where all the parade participants would gather in the parking lot.

The minute Belle arrived with Mr. Big, Mona Lisa ran for her hiding place under my bed. While Laddie and Mr. Big bounced around playfully and Belle and I chatted, I made us toasted cheese sandwiches. I served them with a side of tossed salad and gave the dogs a few mini carrots.

"Should we put their costumes on before we leave or wait until we get there?" I asked my friend after lunch.

"I think it would be better to do it here, before we get into the car. Once they see all the other dogs, they'll be all excited, and you know how Mr. Big wiggles when he's excited."

"Good point." I laughed. "I guess we should go in a few minutes. I'll grab Laddie's lion outfit."

"OK. I'll try to corral Mr. Big," Belle said, reaching for the large tote bag she'd brought, containing Mr. Big's hot dog costume.

Laddie behaved like a perfect gentleman as I put his lion costume on him and adjusted the straps, but Mr. Big was another story. He wiggled so much that Belle struggled to get the little dog into his costume. Once she did, he shook a few times, as though he were trying to shake off water, but he stopped his wiggling when we told him how cute he looked.

Both Laddie and Mr. Big were up for an adventure as we loaded them into the back seat of my SUV and headed out. When we reached the corner by the municipal overflow parking lot, a couple of blocks from the vet clinic, a police officer was directing traffic and waved us into the lot, where we saw many other pet parents with their costumed dogs in tow.

"This must be a bigger event than last year's," Belle said. "Just look at all the dogs! I think we had only about twenty participants last year."

"It's a good thing we came a little bit early. I thought we'd be able to park at the vet's office. Well, here goes," I said, as we opened the back doors and grabbed our dogs' leashes. Raring to go, they jumped down, onto the pavement.

Part of Sagebrush Lane had been blocked off, so all the parade participants walked in the road to the clinic. We saw all kinds of costumed canines, from a chihuahua in a tutu to a Great Dane in a tuxedo. Laddie and Mr. Big pulled mightily on their leashes in their eagerness to join the crowd. We were near a pair of poodles, one miniature and one standard, both wearing glitzy gold sequin vests, and our dogs wanted to make friends with them, but there was no time for schmoozing.

We arrived at the vet clinic's parking lot just as Jerry climbed onto a chair and began shouting instructions to the crowd of parade participants.

His wife Katie and their daughter Kimberly, also a vet, stood beside him with their three dogs, all decked out in clown costumes.

"Jerry, be careful!" Katie cautioned him as he climbed down from the chair, which didn't look all too sturdy.

When she saw us, she waved us over, while Jerry and their daughter took charge of their dogs and got into position to lead the parade.

"Hi, Katie," I said. "I see Jerry's still getting ready for that mountain man reenactment."

"He sure is. Only a couple of weeks now, and then he can shave off that scratchy beard of his. I can't wait!"

We chuckled. Jerry looked like a completely different man with his long hair and bushy beard.

"We didn't realize that the parade was going to be so much bigger than last year's," I said.

"Neither did we! Last Halloween we just took a walk around the block on the sidewalk—no muss, no fuss. Simple. But, by Friday, we'd already had over a hundred people sign up, and we realized parking was going to be a problem. Jerry called his friend who's on the city council, and we found out that we needed a permit to hold the parade. We barely got the paperwork done in time, so it was a good thing he checked. His buddy knows the police chief, and he arranged to barricade the streets to block off our route, and he insisted on providing a police escort to lead the parade. This year, we have to stay off the sidewalks and march in the street."

"What about the visit to the nursing home?" I asked. "I was hoping to see the father of a friend of mine there."

"We can't stop there this year, but you could circle back to see him after the parade's over," Katie told me.

"How will the residents watch the parade?" Belle asked. "Last year we went around back to their patio."

"We've been in touch with the home's director, and she's arranged for the staff to bring the residents who want to see the parade out to their front lawn. It's a little cool today, but not terrible, and they'll all be bundled up, I'm sure. Well, it looks like it's time to get this show on the road. I'd better join Jerry and Kimberly."

Belle and I struggled for a few minutes as our excited dogs strained at their leashes, but, once we began walking, they cooperated nicely as we fell in behind the poodles that had caught their attention earlier. A small crowd lined the street on both sides, and many of them clapped as we passed by. The spectators waved, and we waved back. We'd been cautioned not to stop during the parade, and Jerry had suggested that, if we noticed someone along the route we wanted to see, we do so after the parade had ended.

"Lion!" a toddler, who perched on his father's shoulders, shouted, pointing to Laddie.

"I like the hot dog," we heard his big sister say.

Belle and I both smiled and waved at the kids as we marched past them. As we approached the nursing home, we saw quite a few residents outside, some standing and some in wheelchairs. They clapped loudly and seemed to enjoy the spectacle of over a hundred dogs in their Halloween costumes marching past.

"Amanda! Amanda!" I looked around to see who was calling me and spotted Carrie standing behind her father, who sat in a wheelchair. I hadn't noticed either of them at first. Carrie wore a winter jacket with a hood pulled down over her forehead, and her father, who wore a gray knit cap, was swathed in blankets from head to toe.

Carrie beckoned me to come over, but I shouted that we'd have to come back after the parade. Carrie gave me a thumbs-up sign, so I knew she'd been able to hear me over the noise of the crowd.

"Do you mind if we stop off to see Carrie and her father after the parade?" I asked Belle belatedly since there'd been no time to check with her when I answered Carrie.

"Not at all. I met Carrie at one of the Roadrunner's open houses a few months ago," Belle said, "but I doubt that she'll remember me. It was super busy at the time. Such a shame about her father."

"Yes, it is. I hope he's getting along all right at the nursing home. I'm sure he's going to enjoy seeing the dogs. I noticed that he was smiling at our parade."

Although our route was short, just four blocks, as we circled back to the veterinary clinic, the parade had attracted a lot of attention from the local residents, and there was a satelite truck and reporter from Lonesome Valley's television station ready to interview Jerry when we got back to the staging area in the clinic's parking lot. We saw the station's photographer shooting video, and when he pointed his camera our way, we grinned and waved.

"We'll have to watch the news this evening," Belle said. "We might be on TV."

"Or Mr. Big and Laddie might. It looked like the photographer was pointing his camera at our toes." We both laughed, but we wouldn't think of missing the news tonight. It was fun to live in a town where a pet parade would actually be a story, I mused.

Slowly the crowd began to disperse, the police removed the barriers that had blocked off our parade route, and the spectators returned to their homes. We left the vet clinic's parking lot and walked back to the nursing home on the sidewalk this time, rather than in the street.

I pulled my cell phone out of my jacket pocket and called Carrie to find out where we should meet her. She told me that she'd meet us out front, so we waited near the entry to the lobby until she appeared and showed us to a side door that led to a glassed-in atrium. A group of four, two residents and two visitors, was playing cards on the other side of the room, but aside from the card players, we had the room. Carrie told us she'd go get her father, so we sat on a bench to wait while the dogs, tired after the excitement of marching in a parade with more than a hundred other canines, flopped down beside us.

In a few minutes, Carrie and her father, walking with arms linked, joined us. He didn't seem to be having any problems walking, and I wondered why he'd been in a wheelchair to observe the parade, but then I thought it was probably because he'd have a place to sit while he was watching it.

Carrie settled him in an armchair beside us, and he immediately turned his attention to the dogs, laughing at their costumes and petting them.

"Dad's always been quite a dog lover," Carrie said. "Thanks for coming back to see him, Amanda. You, too, Belle, I remember meeting you last summer at the gallery." She nodded toward her father. "It means a lot to see him happy for a change. He doesn't like living here at all," she whispered.

"It's our pleasure. Mr. Big and Laddie are regular social butterflies," I said. "They love meeting new people."

"I can see that," Carrie chuckled as Mr. Big jumped up onto Carrie's father's lap and Laddie put his paw on Mr. Shaw's knee.

Mr. Big actually stayed put for about five minutes, until the wiggly little dog decided to pay some attention to Belle and jumped down while Laddie lay on the floor and rested his chin on Mr. Shaw's slippered feet.

It wasn't long until Carrie's father complained that he was cold, and Carrie went to his room to get his robe and a blanket.

Mr. Shaw looked at us in confusion, and it was plain to see that he didn't remember who we were, although Carrie had introduced him to us when they came into the atrium earlier. Carrie had confided that he didn't always recognize her, but that didn't seem to be the case today because he perked up when he saw Carrie enter the atrium carrying his blanket.

It wasn't the blanket that attracted my attention, though.

It was the bright red robe that she draped around her father's shoulders.

Chapter 27

I couldn't help but stare at the robe, which was every bit as red as the private detective's Red Riding Hood's costume. I didn't like the thought that was coming into my head. My expression must have changed because Carrie immediately suggested that she and I go into the recreation room to pick up some refreshments and bring them back to the atrium.

Since Belle and Mr. Shaw were playing a game with Mr. Big, and he was running back and forth between them while Laddie sat beside her and watched, she hadn't noticed that I was in a quandary, so when Carrie announced that we'd be back soon with cookies and hot chocolate, Belle just nodded and said "sounds good," without looking up.

As soon as we left the room, Carrie broached the subject head on.

"I know what you're thinking," she said.

"Uh, OK," I murmured, not willing to confront her.

"You think Dad pushed Monique off that balcony, don't you?"

"No, but I was thinking that he has a red robe. Was he wearing it the night of the party?"

"It's the only robe he has." Carrie shrugged. "That doesn't mean anything, though. His nurse already told the police that Dad was asleep at the time."

"Do you happen to know which officer the nurse talked to that night?"

"It was the new guy, Sergeant Boyd, I believe."

"Uh, oh."

"What?"

"Unfortunately, Sergeant Boyd's made several mistakes that even I know about, so I'm not sure his interview skills are up to snuff."

Carrie looked worried. "Dad wouldn't have. . . . He *couldn't*." She hesitated. "Oh, who am I kidding? I don't know what he'd do anymore." She began to sob.

"Maybe we can set your mind at ease," I said. "Let's talk to the nurse who was with him that night."

"All right," Carrie agreed, "but I don't know what I'll do if it turns out that Dad did it. I already feel guilty enough that we left the key to the cupola in plain sight where anybody could grab it."

"There's no way you could have anticipated what would happen, Carrie."

"We should have canceled the party when we had to bring Dad home," she moaned.

I was afraid that, no matter what I said, Carrie's burden of guilt would overwhelm her and her grandmother, who felt equally guilty. Even so, I thought we should try to find out whether Sergeant Boyd had really learned the true story about what happened the night Monique was pushed to her death, so I decided to press ahead.

"How can we get in touch with the nurse?" I asked. "Do you need to contact the agency?"

"No, he only works for the agency part-time, but he works here full-time. In fact, he's the one who suggested this facility."

"Is he here today?" I asked.

"No idea. I guess we can check with the receptionist."

"Let's do that."

We walked down the hallway to the lobby, but we didn't need to make inquiries at the front desk because Carrie spotted the nurse as he came in the front door.

"Hi, Russ, could I talk to you for a minute?" Carrie asked.

"Sure," he replied. "I don't go on duty for half an hour yet."

She quickly introduced us before getting right to the point.

"We need to ask you about last Saturday night," Carrie said.

"What about it?" Russ shifted uneasily. "I already talked to the cops."

"Yes, I know. Sergeant Boyd, right?"

"If you say so. He was a young guy, but I don't remember his name."

"It must have been Boyd," I told Carrie. "He's got to be the youngest officer on the force."

"Could you please tell us exactly what you told him?" Carrie asked.

"Not much to tell. When the lady fell, we were in your dad's room, and he was asleep."

"You're absolutely sure?" I asked.

"Yes," he said firmly, but he didn't look me in the eye.

"OK, well, thanks, Russ." Carrie said.

Russ didn't waste any time beating a hasty departure.

"He was lying, wasn't he?"

I was surprised that Carrie had picked up on Russ's prevarication, but I had to agree with her.

"I certainly got the impression that Russ knows more than he's willing to say. Could he have known Monique himself?"

"I doubt it. He hasn't lived in Lonesome Valley very long, and I know he's been working all the hours he can get, so it doesn't seem very likely."

"Maybe all those long hours were getting to him," I speculated. "I wonder if *he* fell asleep himself the night of the party."

"If so, he's not likely to admit it. People don't hire a private duty nurse to sleep on the job, and his main job was keeping an eye on Dad and seeing to his needs. Alzheimer's or not, I just can't believe that Dad would have anything to do with Monique's death. You know what? He's not in a fog all the time. I'm going to ask him if he remembers anything about that night."

"All right, but first we'd better go grab a tray of cookies and some hot chocolate from the recreation room," I reminded Carrie.

We went to the rec room and quickly assembled a tray of goodies and another with four mugs of hot chocolate. By the time we returned to the atrium, the hot chocolate wasn't so hot anymore, but Carrie said it would be easier for her father to handle the lukewarm drink because he'd spilled hot coffee on himself a couple of times, and she didn't want him to get burned.

"Here we are," she said, setting the tray of hot chocolate on a side table. As soon as she put it down, she handed her father a mug, and I held the tray of cookies while he selected one. Of course, the dogs wanted to get into the act, and they started begging for a cookie.

Neither Belle nor I usually fed the dogs sweet treats, but she'd come prepared. While we munched on our cookies and sipped the tepid chocolate, she doled out a few crunchy dog treats, which she'd hidden in her bag before we left for the parade.

Carrie set her mug down and began scrolling on her cell phone. I wondered what she was doing until she located the picture of Monique she'd taken as, blowing kisses, she was making her grand entrance at Carrie's party.

She showed the picture to her father, and he stared at it. I thought I saw a glimmer of recognition, but I couldn't be sure.

"Dad, have you ever seen this woman?"

"That's Marilyn, Carrie. You ought to know that. Everyone knows Marilyn Monroe."

"Yes, but have you ever seen her in person?"

"'*Gentlemen Prefer Blondes.*'"

"You saw the movie?"

"Sure, I did. We watched it together, remember?"

"Yes, I do," Carrie said, as she quickly wiped a tear away, "but have you seen her lately?"

"That's impossible. Marilyn's dead, Carrie," he declared solemnly.

"Oh, that's right," she said.

Belle passed the tray of cookies around again, and after we'd all helped ourselves and eaten another cookie, I suggested that it was time to make our departure.

"We'll bring Laddie and Mr. Big to see you again, if that's all right, Mr. Shaw."

He nodded and gave each of the dogs a pat.

Keeping an eye on her father, Carrie walked us the few yards to the door.

"See, I told you. He does know what's going on some of the time, and I definitely got the impression that he never saw Monique last Saturday night."

"I agree," I said, "but I suppose it's possible the nurse knows something."

"Well, if he does, I wish he'd tell the cops."

Chapter 28

Laddie and Mr. Big, still sporting their Halloween costumes, headed straight for the car when we left.

"I think we should take pity on them and take their costumes off now," Belle said.

"Yes," I agreed, and I opened the hatchback before we undressed our canine companions and stowed their outfits in the back. "I think they looked adorable, don't you?"

"I certainly do. Even though Mr. Big didn't want to wear his hot dog costume at first, he didn't seem to mind later, especially after the parade started.

"I think Laddie actually likes to wear his lion costume. He always wants to be the center of attention, and it gets him plenty."

We laughed before all piling in my SUV and heading for home.

"What was all that about Marilyn Monroe?" Belle asked once we got going.

"Carrie was trying to find out whether her father saw Monique the night of the party. When I saw his red robe, I did a double-take, and Carrie noticed."

Belle frowned. I could tell she wasn't following me.

"Her dad was at home and staying on the third floor that night," I explained.

"Oh, so he may be a suspect?"'

"I feared so at the time, but now I doubt it because it sounded as though he never saw Monique that night. It was Monique's picture that Carrie showed him, but he only connected it with Marilyn Monroe and the movie she was in when she wore that pink evening gown. Anyway, his nurse told the police that Mr. Shaw was asleep at the time Monique was killed."

"Maybe they should be looking at the nurse. After all, if he was taking care of Carrie's father, he was up there, on the third floor, too."

"I know, and he did act more than a little uncomfortable when Carrie and I were asking him about it this afternoon."

"So that's what took you two so long to come back with the cookies," Belle said.

"Yes. We both thought Russ—that's the nurse's name— was lying about something, but what? My best guess is that he fell asleep himself, and he doesn't want to admit it because he does private duty nursing part-time. If the agency he's with knew that he'd been sleeping on the job, they might cut him loose. Who knows? It's only a guess, but since Carrie told me that Russ has been trying to get as many hours of work as possible in addition to his full-time job at the memory care center, I figured it made sense. We don't believe that he even knew Monique, and, if that's the case, he wouldn't have any reason to shove her off the balcony."

"Are you going to tell Bill that you think Russ lied?"

"Yes, even though he probably doesn't want to hear anything from me. I thought I'd wait until tomorrow because I'm sure he'll show up at Monique's memorial service. Most of the members of the Road-runner will be there, but I'm pretty sure Lieutenant Belmont will show up, too, possibly with Dave or Sergeant Boyd."

"I don't envy you any conversation with Bill Belmont, but maybe you'll luck out and be able to tell Dave, instead."

"That would be fine with me! You know, it's so bizarre to see the grumpy lieutenant acting nice as pie whenever he's around Pamela. It's like he's a different person," I said as I pulled into my garage.

As I opened the door to let the dogs out, Dennis, a big grin on his face, appeared in the doorway. He swooped up Mr. Big and gave Laddie a pat.

"How did the parade go?" he asked Belle.

"Great! Mr. Big and Laddie loved the attention. Some people in the crowd even clapped for them."

"Sorry I missed it."

"You're not sorry at all, mister, or you wouldn't have begged off," Belle said playfully.

Dennis flashed another grin at his wife. "You'll forgive me, won't you?"

"I suppose so," she said pointing at her cheek. Dennis quickly took the hint and planted a kiss there while she giggled, and Mr. Big struggled in Dennis's arms.

After Dennis set the little dog down and grabbed his leash, we waved good-bye, and Laddie and I went inside. Seeing Belle and Dennis together made me think about Brian's absence this weekend, and I hoped I'd hear from him soon. I was eager to find out about the shake-up at his company and his reaction to the meeting.

It was around eight o'clock when he finally called with an apology. He'd been so busy attending meetings and new equipment demonstrations that he'd felt as though he'd barely had time to breathe.

"I finally feel good about my job again," Brian told me. "The CEO knows his stuff, and he's already replaced some people who were doing more harm than good with their micro-managing. Plus, he's promised to give the site managers more autonomy. As long as we're doing our jobs, we won't have to worry about being second-guessed on every little decision we make. And you should see some of the fantastic innovations in equipment that are coming soon."

"Brian, that's great. I'm so happy for you."

"Thanks; it was touch and go there for a while. I almost called a headhunter last week to see about getting a different job, so I'm pleased that I didn't have to go that far. It's a whole new ball game now, and what a relief it is to have somebody in charge who actually knows the business."

He sounded just like the old Brian, again, enthusiastic about his job. I knew how stressed he'd felt during the last several months, even to the point that he'd acted rather irritable a few times, which wasn't like him at all. I had a feeling we'd dodged a bullet.

When he asked about how the pet parade had gone, I told him that Dennis had ducked out because Brian couldn't be there, too.

"I'll have to give him a hard time about that next weekend," Brian said.

"You won't be the first. Belle's already done a pretty good job of it." It felt good to have a light-hearted moment as we laughed together.

It was no laughing moment when we discussed Monique's untimely demise, though. Brian told me he'd had nightmares about her falling from the balcony at Carrie's house, and I admitted that I had, too.

"If only we could have seen what happened from a different angle," I said. "We might have been able to spot the killer."

"Maybe Carrie's neighbor Patricia did see whoever it was, but since she wasn't wearing her glasses, I suppose whatever she could see was a blur. I never really thought about it much, since I'm not near-sighted myself, but my assistant is, and she can't see past her desk without her glasses on. They're really thick, too."

"But she can see colors, right?"

"Sure."

"As far as I know, the red flash of color that Patricia saw is the only clue the police have, unless they were able to get some information from Monique's phone, but they wouldn't reveal what they found, if they did discover something."

After I told Brian about Mr. Shaw's red robe and our conversation with the nurse, we proceeded to rehash the possible motives of all the people we knew who had worn red the night of the costume party, but we came up with more questions than answers.

"The memorial service for Monique is tomorrow," I said. "I'm sure most of the members of the Roadrunner will be there, along with the police."

"I'd come with you if I could."

"I know you would. At least you'll be able to come home this weekend, though."

"And every weekend from now on, now that I won't have any corporate bigwigs throwing a monkey wrench in the works at the last minute. See you Saturday. No, on second thought, make that Friday night. What would you say to a late dinner after your studio tour's over?"

"I'd say 'hooray'! You're on!"

Chapter 29

The gray skies matched my gloomy mood as I dressed in a navy blue wool blazer and charcoal gray pants for Monique's memorial service the next day. Even Laddie seemed affected by the dreary weather. He wasn't his usual bouncy self, and he'd been snoozing most of the day. Mona Lisa had scampered under my bed the minute Emma left the house in the morning and hadn't come out since.

The memorial service for Monique was scheduled to take place in the chapel at Lonesome Valley Funeral Home, and Susan and I planned to meet there so that we could sit together.

After I transferred a few things from my large everyday tote bag into a small navy leather purse, I was ready to go. When I grabbed my car keys from the kitchen counter and headed for the door, Laddie accompanied me. After I told him to be a good boy and began to pull the door closed, he gave a mighty yawn, and I knew he'd resume his nap as soon as I pulled out of the garage.

When I arrived at the funeral home, I drove around and parked in the home's lot in back of the building where I waited a few minutes until I spotted Susan's car coming. She must have seen me at about the same time, and she parked in the empty spot next to my SUV.

"I stopped by the Roadrunner on the way, and our two newest members are holding down the fort," Susan said, "although I doubt they'll have to deal with much business this afternoon. They told me Pamela's planning to go back there to close at five."

"I think most of the members will be attending the service, don't you?"

"Most of them. Several people have to work, so they won't be here."

"That includes Valerie and Frank, which is probably a good thing, considering that Monique's return to the Roadrunner caused a rift between them. I still can't believe how clueless Frank's acted ever since Monique came back to town."

"I know. He's always seemed so steady, and he's not the flirtatious type like someone else we know."

I realized she was talking about her nephew Chip, who, coincidentally, we found waiting for us around front, next to the door.

"I wish there was no need to be here today. If only I'd stayed with Monique during the party," Chip said, "she'd still be alive. She wanted to see Carrie's studio, and I didn't see her again until. . . ."

"Chip, you shouldn't blame yourself," Susan told him.

"No, you definitely shouldn't," I agreed. "There was absolutely no reason to think that Monique was in danger."

"Wasn't there? What about that private eye who scared her half to death? I'm telling you, Monique was really frightened of her."

"Of course, being harassed is no fun, but surely the woman had been hired to dig up some kind of information, rather than harm Monique, don't you think?" Although I wanted to try to reassure Chip that Monique's death hadn't been his fault, I wasn't a hundred percent sure about the PI's motives or how far she'd go to do her job for her employer, who I presumed was Edward McCall's daughter.

"I suppose," Chip said glumly. "I felt totally helpless when we saw Monique fall."

"We all did, but I know you were a comfort to her in her last moments," I said as Susan put her arm around her nephew and gave him a squeeze. All three of us teared up, and I reached into my purse for a tissue to dab my eyes as Chip quickly brushed the back of his hand across his face and Susan blinked back her tears.

"I suppose we'd better go find a seat," Susan said when the moment had passed.

Chip opened the door for us, and we all stepped inside.

A few people were waiting in the reception area, Pamela among them, but Chip steered us past her and down the hallway to the chapel before we had a chance to greet her. I didn't think Pamela had noticed, though, because she'd had her back turned to us at the time, while she talked to a couple I didn't recognize.

"Don't tell me you and Pamela are still on the outs," Susan said.

"I'm afraid so. She's not too happy with me, even though I told her why I removed Monique's pastels from the gallery wall. Pamela insisted that I hang them all back, just the way they were when I took them down. I couldn't remember the arrangement exactly, and that seemed to make Pamela even madder. She hasn't spoken to me since. I sent her flowers as kind of a good will gesture, but she didn't call me, like she usually would. I bet those roses are sitting in her trash can right now."

"Oh, Chip. . . ." Susan murmured.

I resolved to have a word later with Pamela about the situation. After all, she and Chip had been the best of friends, and his reason for hiding Monique's pastels was understandable, even if ill-advised.

A solemn young woman dressed in a black suit handed us each a printed program with a lovely picture of Monique on the front. She looked so young and lively that it was difficult to believe that she was gone.

As we walked down the center aisle of the small chapel, we noticed that several mourners had already taken their seats. We settled on a place a few rows back from the front, and Susan slid across the wooden bench while I followed, and Chip sat at the end on the aisle. I hadn't noticed Lieutenant Belmont or any other police officers there yet, but I was sure they'd show up soon.

Carrie and her grandmother Betty were the next to arrive. After they sat down in the row ahead of us, both women turned around to greet us. But when Betty saw Dorothy coming down the center aisle with Dawn, Betty turned back and looked the other way while Dorothy gestured to an empty row on the right side of the aisle and made her way to the end and Dawn followed her. Her action reminded me that the two had something of a feud going, and I supposed that the seat on the end was as far away from Betty as Dorothy was able to go, given that she and her daughter had already come up the center aisle, so if they'd backtracked, it would have looked rather strange.

It wasn't long before the chapel was almost full. I turned around to scan the crowd, most of whom were members of the Roadrunner, although there were several people I didn't recognize, too.

I spotted Lieutenant Belmont leaning against the back wall. He wasn't taking notes, but I knew he was mentally registering every person who came in. I thought perhaps he'd sit with Pamela when the service started, but, after a brief conversation with Pamela and Ralph, the lieutenant stayed put while they proceeded to walk to the front and sit down in the first row. In a minute, one of the funeral home employees ushered Monique's cousin Faye to a seat next to them. I was sure the seating arrangement had been made ahead of time. I had a vague recollection that Pamela had mentioned something about Faye's asking her to say a few words at the service.

Strangely, Faye's husband was nowhere to be seen, but, once Faye had been seated, Brooks materialized and took a place next to her in the front pew. I wondered whether she had asked Brooks to say a few words, too.

I'd noticed that the usher who brought Faye in had first removed a velvet rope that had been placed across the row to show that it was reserved. There was still a rope on the right front row, but the pastor had already appeared to lead the service, and that row was still empty.

As the minister began to speak about celebrating Monique's life, we could hear people talking in the back. I turned and saw Todd Whitman, dressed in a conservative dark suit and tie, with two couples, both much more casually dressed in jeans.

The minister paused, and the little group suddenly noticed that everybody was looking their way.

Todd looked embarrassed and mumbled an apology before the five of them marched to the front, removed the velvet rope from across the right front row, and sat down.

As soon as they'd settled into the front pew, the minister resumed his announcement and then led a prayer, followed by a hymn. Then he turned to Todd and said that Mr. Whitman would present a tribute to Monique, before stepping back while Todd took his place behind the pulpit.

"We lost my fiancée Monique far too soon," Todd said.

Susan and I looked at each other, and she raised her eyebrow. From what Todd had told Brooks, Brian, and me, the two had never been engaged, although Todd had said that he was sure she would have married him in time. Perhaps his assumption had been wishful thinking, but I supposed he could be excused for indulging in it, considering what might have been, at Monique's memorial service.

"Monique was well known socially in Palm Springs, but what many of her acquaintances didn't realize was that she was an exceptionally talented artist. Her dream was to have her own gallery." He choked as he went on: "Someone took that dream away from her."

Silence reigned as Todd bowed his head and struggled to get his emotions under control. Finally he looked up and continued. "Today, I'd like to pay a final tribune to my dear Monique." He nodded to one of the men who'd been sitting with him in the front row, and, a few seconds later, a large screen descended from its recessed slot in the ceiling.

For about ten minutes, we watched as a professionally produced and narrated glimpse into Monique's life as an artist unfolded on the screen. We saw Monique entering her studio, which appeared to be a separate building, which I assumed was on Edward McCall's property in Palm Springs. Images of Monique at work with her pastels followed in quick succession. I couldn't help but admire her deft technique. She'd certainly been on the path to wider recognition.

The film went on to show Monique at the reception for the opening of a show she'd had at a gallery in Palm Springs. Not surprisingly, men flocked around her as she laughed and sipped champagne. Although Edward McCall was nowhere in sight, Todd appeared at her side and didn't leave her.

The video ended with a tour of the one-woman show featuring Monique's pastels before the narrator, whose rich baritone voice I was sure I'd heard before, solemnly intoned a poem while the scene switched from the gallery to waves crashing on a beach and the camera panned into the sunset.

As I looked around the chapel, dabbing my eyes, I thought the phrase "not a dry eye in the house" couldn't have captured the moment any better.

When I glanced down, I noticed that the poem was the same one printed below Monique's photo on the memorial program:

Our lives, like waves that
cross
The vast sea's depths, to
toss
And break upon the
beach,
Are heralds, come to teach
That artists' lives subside
Soon after they arise—
But their works' great
beauty
Lasts an eternity,
And the fond memory

They leave for us to see,
In painted mementos
Of their lives lost, disclose
To the world they depart,
The passion of their art,
A devotion that can
Mortality withstand.
Her every work of art,
Recalls to mind and heart
The loveliness of fair
Artiste Monique d'Albert.

Todd had gone back to his seat in the front row when the film started, and after the screen was raised, the pastor announced that Monique's cousin Faye would speak.

Poor Faye looked as though she wasn't going to get too far. Her face wet with tears, she stumbled over her first words as she unfolded a paper and read from it. "Monique and I lost our parents in a horrible accident," she said. "We had only each other." Faye managed to read most of the short tribute, which focused mainly on remembrances of times they'd shared when their parents were still alive, before she began sobbing.

Chapter 30

Returning to her seat, Faye handed the paper to Brooks, who took over and finished reading it for her.

I thought Pamela might be next to speak, but it was Ralph who, aided by his cane, rose and said a few words about Monique's artistic talents and the beauty of her pastels.

After Ralph finished, the pastor asked if anyone would like to share a memory, but nobody volunteered to speak extemporaneously, perhaps because it would have been extremely difficult to follow the slick Hollywood production that Todd had presented earlier.

More prayers and songs followed before the minister wrapped up the service with a reading of the Twenty-Third Psalm. Then an usher appeared promptly and escorted everyone who'd been sitting in the first row down the center aisle to the chapel door.

As Faye walked by, Betty pointed to her, then turned to her granddaughter and whispered, "They always bring a big crew, so I can't be absolutely sure, but I think she's one of our cleaners."

"You mean Monique's cousin?" Carrie asked.

"Yes. I think I recognize her. She's not one of the regular crew, but they have a lot of subs."

"Hmm. I never noticed. I guess I'm usually in the studio when they're working."

Both women rose when the usher came to clear their row. On the other side, Dawn and Dorothy were preparing to depart, too. I couldn't believe that Betty deliberately waited for Dorothy and grabbed her arm. I feared that a terrible scene was about to unfold, and I held my breath, but to my surprise Betty said, "I owe you an apology."

Taken aback, Dorothy just stared at her former friend.

Betty continued, "I'm sorry. I've behaved like a fool. Can you ever forgive me?"

Dorothy broke into a huge smile and gave her a big hug.

The two walked down the aisle together, followed by Carrie and Dawn, who discreetly bumped fists.

"I'm glad those two made up," Susan said. "Maybe it took attending a funeral for Betty to understand how silly she was acting. It's certainly a reminder that we may not have as much time as we think, so we'd better make the most of it when we can."

Monique had most likely thought she'd had all the time in the world, but it had come to a bitter end for no apparent reason. Whatever motives people may have had to kill her didn't seem to be very strong, in my opinion, which made me wonder whether the murder had been premeditated or a spur-of-the-moment action, perhaps by someone who now regretted having pushed Monique to her death.

As we left the chapel, emerging into the funeral home's reception area, we saw that Faye, Brooks, and Todd had formed a line and were thanking everyone for attending as they filed out of the chapel, into the funeral home's reception area.

Faye was first in line, which meant that Brooks and Todd stood next to each other, and I had the distinct impression that neither of them was too happy about it. I wondered if jealousy had reared its ugly head, but there was no telling. Both men behaved politely, if not quite cordially.

Although a few people had left already, others stood around in small groups. Most were speaking in hushed tones, but Todd's friends were the exception. They had gathered in a corner and, every once in a while, a peal of laughter rang out. Then one of the men was interrupted by the insistent buzz of his cell phone.

"You're kidding, right?" he asked, in a voice loud enough for us to hear.

Whoever had called him must have been on speaker mode. "See if you can get him to take care of it, OK?" the man on the other end said.

"No problem. Will do." He hung up with a good-bye and gestured to Todd, who joined the little group, but they were no longer speaking loudly enough for everybody in the room to hear; in fact, the man who'd motioned to Todd appeared to be whispering to him. Todd nodded his head vigorously, slapped him on the back, and his voice ratcheted up a notch. Soon, they were all laughing again, and Todd was inviting them to join him later for dinner at Cabo, one of the restaurants at the Resort. The five left without a backward glance; Todd didn't even speak to Faye before he exited.

When I noticed Lieutenant Belmont next to the door, observing the scene, I decided it was now or never. While Susan joined Pamela and Ralph, I edged my way over to the grumpy detective.

"Lieutenant, could I please have a word? I came across some information yesterday."

"Not now," he told me, waving me off. "I'm working." He pushed off the wall he'd been leaning against and left me standing there while he approached a woman, dressed in black, complete with a hat and veil, who'd been standing alone, observing the other mourners. He spoke to her briefly before leading her toward the exit.

As they passed me on their way out the door of the funeral home, I caught a whiff of the odor of cigarette smoke, which must have been clinging to the woman's attire.

I took a second look at her, and she was close enough when she went by that I could see, even through her heavy veil, that it was the private investigator who'd been dogging Monique before her death.

Todd's departure hadn't broken up the reception line, but Faye and Brooks soon finished thanking everyone who came out of the chapel, and they began talking to Pamela and Susan as soon as Ralph took his leave. Since Lieutenant Belmont had brushed me off, I joined them.

"Who was that woman in black who just left with the cop?" Faye asked me. "Could you tell?"

"Yes, I recognized her. She's that private detective who's been hanging around."

"Why's she still in town? She came over to the house when Monique was staying with us and wanted to talk to her, but Monique wouldn't go to the door. The woman wouldn't take 'no' for an answer from me, but Grant set her straight, and she took off. Haven't seen her since. She's got some nerve showing up here."

"I wonder if Monique knew what the PI was after," I said.

Faye shrugged. "She thought the woman was trying to track down her assets for McCall's daughter, but that doesn't make sense. Monique didn't have much of anything left, other than her artwork.

She pawned all her jewelry, except for one ring and her diamond stud earrings, before she left Palm Springs. The earrings are definitely worth a few thousand, but not the topaz ring—she only kept it because she always did like pink. So I guess it had to be about Monique's pastels." Faye turned to Pamela. "Have you sold any of them?"

Faye's question put Pamela in an awkward position since Todd, not Faye, was the executor of Monique's will. Even though Todd had mentioned to me that Monique's will didn't necessarily preclude his giving some of Monique's assets to her cousin, he wasn't obligated to do so, and he hadn't made any promises that I was aware of.

"Yes, a few," she said, probably because she often posted photos of artwork that had been sold at the Roadrunner on social media, so sales weren't exactly a big secret.

"How much?"

"Pardon me?"

"How much did they sell for?" Faye asked.

"Oh, I couldn't recall the exact figures offhand," Pamela answered.

"Well, ballpark, then," Faye pressed.

I could tell from Pamela's expression that she was uncomfortable with the conversation, not only because Pamela would be reporting the sales figures to Todd, not Faye, but also because discussing the prices that the late artist's work had fetched at her memorial service bordered on appalling and was, no doubt, inappropriate, at the least.

"I'm sure you can get the numbers from Todd," I said, interrupting in an attempt to save Pamela from having to deal with Faye's questions. "But the numbers aren't compiled until a few days after the first of the month for the previous period."

"That's right," Susan agreed. "By the way, we're so sorry that your husband wasn't able to attend today's service."

Susan's attempt to turn the tables on Faye met with some success as Faye had enough sense to look a bit embarrassed.

"Yes, me, too. He wanted to be here," she said. "Unfortunately, he had a schedule to keep, and he couldn't get a substitute driver to fill in."

Her comment left us all in confusion since none of us had any idea what Faye's husband Grant did for a living.

"He's a truck driver," she explained. "He drives a regular route between Phoenix and Las Vegas for one of the big supermarket chains," she continued.

"Well, it's a shame he couldn't be here with you," Susan said, "but it was a lovely service."

Faye stared at the floor for several seconds, and there were tears in her eyes when she looked up. Sad as the occasion was, at least her current behavior better reflected the circumstances than had her insistence on finding out how much money her cousin's artwork had brought in since Monique's death.

We were spared from continuing the conversation when the woman in the dark suit who'd handed us a memorial program when we'd first entered the funeral home appeared to ask Faye whether she'd like the flowers that people had sent to the service to be delivered to the Lonesome Valley Hospital or one of the local nursing homes.

She appeared to be considering what to do and didn't answer immediately.

"Can I take them home?" she finally asked, uncertain as to protocol.

"Of course, if you'd prefer," the woman answered, barely controlling the slight sneer in her voice. "I can arrange to have them brought to your house. There's just a small fee for delivery."

"Oh, no," Faye said, shaking her head. "I'll take them with me in my car."

"Very well, madam," the woman replied, without offering any further assistance.

Faye looked to be at a loss as the woman turned on her heel, leaving Faye to haul all the arrangements out to her car herself.

"We'll give you a hand," I volunteered. "Why don't you bring your car around front while we pick up the flowers?"

"OK, thanks, I'll do that," Faye said with relief. She dug her car keys out of her purse and headed out the door.

Luckily, none of the floral arrangements was so huge that one person couldn't manage it easily. After Pamela, Susan, and I each made a trip carrying flowers outside to Faye's car, some of the other Roadrunner members who hadn't left yet noticed what we were doing and pitched in to assist. With their help, we completed our task in a few minutes, and Faye departed, her car loaded with flowers.

"Strange woman," Pamela commented as we watched her leave.

"She sure is," Susan agreed.

Chapter 31

As Laddie and I set out on our walk the following morning, it occurred to me that I'd put off buying Halloween candy, and, now that the day had arrived, the larder was bare—of Halloween handouts, that is. I was scheduled for a half-day at the Roadrunner, from nine to one, so I could hit the grocery store on the way home, but I doubted that the selection would be too good by then, or even now, for that matter. I was a little surprised that Emma hadn't mentioned needing to stock up, either, but she'd had plenty of work to do over the past few days, studying for exams, so perhaps it hadn't been on her radar, either.

When we returned from our walk, I saw Emma peeping out the window, watching for Matt to arrive to pick her up for the drive to Flagstaff.

"Leaving early today?"

"Yes. Matt wants to drop his car off for an oil change in Flagstaff before we go to class. Since the auto service place is close to the campus, we can walk over and pick the car up this afternoon."

"Are you still planning on being home this evening?"

"Uh, sure, I guess."

"Halloween?"

"Oh! I can't believe I *totally* forgot today is Halloween. Definitely, I'll be here; I'll help you hand out candy. You're going to dress Laddie up in his lion costume, aren't you?"

"You bet. He loves to dress up, and I think the neighborhood kids will get a kick out of seeing him in his outfit."

"I bought a little something for Mona Lisa, too, but I'm afraid she's not going to thank me for making her put it on."

"You'd better do it early before the trick-or-treaters start to arrive, so we can take her picture. I'm sure she won't tolerate whatever it is, so she won't have it on very long."

"I know, but she'll be so cute in it, for a minute, anyway. I suppose she'll hide under the bed for the rest of the evening. You know how she hates a commotion."

Pulling the curtain aside, I said, "Looks like Matt just pulled up."

"OK, gotta run. See you later, Mom. Oh, do we have any candy?"

"None at all. Don't worry. I'll take care of it. You'd better get going."

Emma stuffed her laptop in her backpack and ran out the front door. Matt jumped out and opened the passenger side door for her. Then, they both turned and gave me a quick wave.

"Hmm. Maybe I should go out and pick up some candy now, before it's all gone." Laddie looked at me and cocked his head. I would have taken him with me, but he couldn't go into the store, and I would never leave him alone in the car, even though the cool weather permitted. "Sorry, boy, I have to leave, but Mommy will be back in a flash."

Emma had left a pot of coffee, so I poured a bit in a mug and gulped a little before I left. I was kicking myself all the way to the supermarket for forgetting to buy Halloween treats earlier. At the stroke of seven, I was the very first customer in the door, and I was happy to see that there was a huge Halloween candy display right in the front, near the registers. I grabbed several bags, probably way more than I needed, but I told myself it would be better to have too much than not enough for the costumed munchkins who'd be showing up at our front door tonight.

Since there was a checker on duty, I hurriedly dumped the bags of candy onto the conveyor belt, next to her register, rather than using the self-checkout.

"Getting ready for tonight, I see," she commented cheerfully.

"Yes, I waited till the last minute. I was relieved to see that you still have a lot of Halloween candy on hand."

"Our candy display will be almost bare by this evening, if last year's sellout is any predictor. You were wise to come early in the day," she said, as she bagged my purchases.

I tapped my credit card on the reader, and the checker plucked my receipt from her printer and tucked it into one of my bags.

"Happy Halloween!" she said.

"Happy Halloween to you, too. I hope you're not too swamped."

"Nature of the beast," she said with a smile.

When I got home, Laddie greeted me as though I'd just returned from a long trip to Siberia. "It's OK, Laddie. Mommy wasn't gone long. Let's have some breakfast."

My eager canine panted in excitement while I put some dog food in his bowl. I expected Mona Lisa to show up, too, but she was snoozing in the corner of the sofa, so I'd have to feed her later. No way was I going to leave her cat food out for Laddie to sample.

While Laddie chowed down, I fixed myself a bowl of cereal and finally had a full cup of coffee. When I'd finished, I saw that Mona Lisa was stirring, so I rattled the bag of cat food, and she ran to the kitchen and pressed herself against my ankles until I put her bowl down for her and shooed Laddie into the living room so that Mona Lisa could breakfast in peace.

Laddie was happy enough to have my undivided attention for a few minutes as he sat beside me and I petted him. I'd be leaving him again soon, to go to the Roadrunner, but this time he wouldn't mind because he'd be spending my shift with Mr. Big and Belle.

As soon as Mona Lisa finished, I left the pet "siblings" to their own devices while I showered and dressed for a morning at the gallery. I still hadn't spoken to Pamela about forgiving Chip for concealing Monique's pastels, so I figured this morning would be a good time to do it. Also, I'd never told Lieutenant Belmont that I suspected Mr. Shaw's nurse might be hiding some information about the night Monique died. I might try to call him after I spoke to Pamela, if we weren't busy, which was quite likely to be the case on a Tuesday morning.

When I entered the gallery at a few minutes before nine, Pamela was standing next to the register, but Ralph, who was also scheduled to work in the morning, was nowhere in sight. It seemed like a good time to talk to Pamela about Chip, but, before I had the chance, Chip came into the gallery himself. As soon as Pamela saw him, she turned around, marched down the hall to her office, and closed the door.

"Uh, oh," Chip muttered. "I switched shifts with Ralph because I was hoping to talk to her."

"I was planning on having a chat with her, too. I thought I'd try to get her to lighten up on you."

"No luck, huh?"

"I just got here. I haven't had a chance yet."

"Well, this is ridiculous. I'm guess I'm going to have to have it out with her."

"No, Chip! Don't give her a hard time. She's been through too much this year."

"I don't intend to. I should have said 'grovel.' I'm going to beg her to forgive me, even if I have to get down on my knees to do it."

Chip walked purposefully down the hall and knocked on Pamela's office door, but he didn't wait for an invitation to enter. He didn't close the door, either, but the two weren't speaking very loudly, and I couldn't hear their conversation. Meanwhile, I did the morning dusting and double checked that the cash register was set up for the day.

It was at least half an hour before Pamela and Chip joined me at the cash wrap. Thankfully, it was obvious that they had made up.

"I hope Lieutenant Belmont didn't give you too much grief over your report that the Roadrunner had been broken into," Chip said.

"No, he didn't blame me. He did urge me to go ahead with some enhanced security, though; I was going to drop that idea after I found out what had really happened, but he convinced me it would be a good idea to do it anyway, even though it'll put a dent in our budget."

Chip had the grace to look down when Pamela mentioned 'what had really happened.'"

"That's amazing, Pamela," I said. "I mean that the lieutenant didn't give you a hard time over making a police report about a crime when there wasn't one."

"I know how you and Susan feel about him, Amanda—you, too, Chip—but Bill's not such a bad guy. He's never acted unpleasant toward me, not even when he arrested me."

Pamela seemed entirely clueless about the reason the lieutenant acted like a different man around her, and, though I suspected he was attracted to her, I didn't think it was a good idea to inform her about my opinions. I could be mistaken about the lieutenant's motives, but I didn't think so. I'd certainly seen his other, grumpier side, often enough. I couldn't help but think about his rudeness to Belle when we'd run into him when he came to Nancy's house to search for Monique's cell phone. In any case, I was glad that the lieutenant wasn't treating Pamela the way he treated most other people.

"That's good, Pamela," Chip said. He wasn't likely to bad mouth the lieutenant now, not after just having resolved his differences with Pamela.

An insistent, but muffled, beeping noise alerted me that my phone was ringing. I'd stashed it in the deep bottom drawer, under the counter, so it took me a few seconds to open both the drawer and my purse and dig my phone out.

"You take the morning paper, don't you?" Susan asked after she'd said 'good morning'."

"No, I don't. Belle and Dennis subscribe, so I see it sometimes, but I'm at the Roadrunner this morning. I can borrow it later from Belle if there's something of interest in it."

"There certainly is, and you might want to look at it sooner rather than later. See if you can get a copy downtown, and check out the legal notices on page eight. Oops, I have to run. My student's just arriving for her watercolors lesson. I'll talk to you later."

I turned back to Pamela and Chip. "Did you hear that?"

"No, what's up?" Chip asked.

"Susan said to check the legal notices in the paper this morning. I don't suppose either one of you has a copy."

"I never look at a newspaper myself," Chip said, "but you subscribe, don't you, Pamela?"

"Yes, but I haven't so much as glanced at it this morning, and I didn't bring it with me. Why don't I run next door and buy a copy?"

"I'll go," Chip said, "and I'll get us all a latte while I'm at it. Any special orders, or will it be the usual?"

"The usual," Pamela and I said in unison, and then we giggled while a broad grin spread across Chip's face. I was glad Pamela and Chip had patched up their differences over Chip's impulsive action to protect Monique's pastels from possible danger.

"Has Lieutenant Belmont said anything to you about what the private eye was doing at Monique's memorial service yesterday?" I asked, hoping that the lieutenant had filled her in.

"No, I haven't seen him since the service," Pamela told me. "Strange that she was there."

"Yes, it was the odor of stale cigarettes when she walked by that tipped me off. Otherwise, I wouldn't have realized the woman in the heavy black veil was none other than the investigator who keeps hanging around."

"She was obviously trying to disguise herself because she knew she wouldn't be welcome. I wonder why she came."

"I suppose for the same reason she's been hanging around; she must be trying to pick up some tidbit of information for Edward McCall's daughter. It does seem odd, though, considering that Monique never filed a lawsuit contesting his will. I guess she may still be concerned that Todd could file one on behalf of Monique's estate. He's already admitted that Monique had no case, but maybe Nicole McCall doesn't know that yet."

"Very strange, if you ask me."

We continued to speculate about the private detective until Pamela noticed that it had been quite a while since Chip had left the gallery.

"What do you suppose is taking Chip so long?" she asked. "The Coffee Klatsch isn't usually so slow."

"Could be they're having trouble with one of their coffee makers," I surmised. "I can go next door and check."

"Oh, that's all right. Whatever the holdup is, I'm sure Chip will get back as soon as he can."

About five minutes later, Chip finally returned to the gallery, carrying a cardboard container with three cups. We could see a folded newspaper under his arm, too.

"Sorry it took so long," he said, as he placed the cardboard container on top of the counter and handed us each a latte. "The Coffee Klatsch was sold out of papers, so I had to run down to the Bread Bowl to find one." He set the newspaper beside the cardboard container.

"No wonder you didn't come back right away," Pamela said to Chip. Turning to me, she added, "What do you suppose could be so important that Susan wanted you to look at it right away?"

"I don't know," I said, "but we're about to find out."

Chapter 32

I unfolded the paper and spread it out on the countertop.

"Here we go," I said, turning to page eight. "The print's so tiny I'm surprised anybody looks at these legal notices."

"I doubt many people do," Pamela commented, as we all scanned the page.

"What are we supposed to be looking for?" Chip asked.

"I'm not sure. Susan just said to check page eight."

"There!" Pamela said, pointing to one of the notices. "This must be it. See—Faye Stanhope."

We stared at the page in an attempt to decipher the notice's legalese.

"What does it mean?" Chip asked. "I can't make heads or tails out of this notice."

"Faye's filed for probate, Chip," Pamela explained. "She wants to be named the administrator of Monique's estate. That's like an executor, someone with the responsibility of locating heirs, determining assets, and settling any outstanding debts."

"Wow! You sound like a lawyer," Chip said. "Wait a minute. I thought Todd Whitman was Monique's executor."

"So he says, but has he given you any paperwork that would prove it, Pamela?" I asked.

"No, but he told me he'd mail the paperwork to me this week. He was planning on filing for probate in California, after he returns to Palm Springs."

"Looks like Faye beat him to it. Since Monique died here, in Lonesome Valley, and what few possessions she had were also here, maybe Arizona has jurisdiction. I guess that's one for the courts to sort out. Do you suppose Todd got wind of what Faye was doing yesterday? I noticed that they didn't speak to each other at all, not even when they were both in the reception line."

"No, they didn't," Pamela agreed, "and it was almost like they were making a point of sitting on opposite sides of the aisle in the chapel."

"Is Faye after Monique's pastels?" Chip asked.

"Good question," I said. "Monique had her pastels, a pair of diamond earrings, a topaz ring, and not much else but the clothes she brought with her, but Faye did seem to be focused on those pastels. Yesterday, she insisted on finding out how much Faye's artwork had brought in this month, and she didn't drop it until Susan distracted her.

"I remember something else now, too. My friends Rebecca and Greg Winter knew Monique when she was in the same high school class as their daughter. By the way, they said her name was Mona Albert back then; she changed it later. Anyway, they told me that her cousin had destroyed some of Monique's artwork when they were in high school."

"Maybe Monique thought it could happen again. Could be that's why she wanted me to protect her pastels," Chip said. "After she told me to 'save her pastels,' she said, 'please don't let them be destroyed.'"

"Are you sure she didn't say anything else?" I asked.

Chip shook his head. "Nothing else about the art. She was having trouble breathing."

"That's right. We all heard her murmur 'air,' but could it be that she was saying 'heir'? You know, as in 'inheritance.'"

"Air or heir," Pamela said. "It does sound the same. Do you think she meant Faye?"

"I do. As far as we know, Faye's her only living relative, but her cousin could have been on her mind for another reason."

"What's that?" Chip asked.

"Faye could have been the last person Monique saw before she was pushed over the balcony."

"You mean. . . ."

"Faye could be the killer."

Chapter 33

"We need to call Bill," Pamela said, but before I could respond, a group of several women entered the gallery, and we automatically moved to assist them.

"This gallery is fabulous," one of the visitors commented as she and the others looked around. "Every bit as good as any in Scottsdale."

"We're happy you like it," Pamela said graciously. "Let us know if you have any questions."

"I do," a tiny woman with blue curls piped up. "I've been here before, and I like these Western landscapes." She pointed toward one of Ralph's paintings. "But they're so expensive I can't afford an original. Does this artist Ralph Anderson ever sell any prints?"

"I'm afraid we don't carry any prints in the gallery," Pamela told her. Seeing the look of disappointment on the woman's face, she added, "but he does sometimes have a few prints available at shows. Would you like me to call him and check on it for you?"

"Oh, would you? That would be great."

"Of course, I'll call him right now."

While Pamela went to the cash wrap to call Ralph, Chip and I interacted with the other potential customers, and I soon found myself behind the glass display counter where we kept the jewelry, showing pieces to a couple of them. I was vaguely aware of Chip's conversing with another woman who was looking for floral art as he led her around the Roadrunner and pointed out paintings she might like.

I was ringing up sales for some of Carrie's earrings and one of her large turquoise pendant necklaces when I saw Ralph pull up in front in his big pickup truck. As soon as Chip noticed that our oldest member was struggling with two large framed prints, he rushed outside and took them. Ralph had his cane with him, and he leaned on it heavily as he hobbled into the gallery with Chip at his side.

Chip placed the prints against the wall, underneath Ralph's original paintings, and we all gathered around. Ralph explained that he'd sold the originals of the two prints he'd brought years ago, so they were no longer on display in the gallery.

"But these are perfect!" the woman who'd asked whether prints were available exclaimed. "I can only buy one, though, and I can't decide which."

"Mavis, don't you think this one with the purple mountains in the background would look great hanging over the sofa in your living room?" one of the other women asked. "That is where you were thinking of displaying it, isn't it?"

"Yes, and you're right, Arlene." She clapped her hands. "I'll take it. Oh, I forgot to ask how much it costs." A shadow of a frown crossed her face.

Ralph quickly assessed the situation and quoted her a price that I knew was much lower than what he would normally sell a print of that size at a show, but her eyes lit up when she heard the number, and she reached into her purse and pulled out her wallet.

"Let's go over here," Pamela suggested, leading her toward the cash register, "and we'll take care of the transaction."

While Pamela rang up the sale, and Ralph chatted with his buyer, Chip carefully wrapped the framed print in sturdy paper and added a couple of layers of bubble wrap.

"I'd like to buy your other print," Arlene said to Ralph, "if it costs the same as the one Marvis bought."

He readily agreed to the sale, and Pamela and Chip went back to work processing the transaction and preparing the framed artwork so that it could be moved without damaging it. A smile on his face, Ralph ducked out as soon as the print was ready to go to its new owner.

We had two more sales after that, both for Monique's framed pastels. Although they were the smallest and least expensive of her artwork, the total still came to nearly a thousand dollars.

The group departed with their purchases, but the sale of Monique's pastels certainly reminded us of our previous conversation.

"Tell us again why you think Faye killed her cousin," Chip said. "Is it all about jealousy?"

"That's certainly a big part of it," I said. "We know Faye and Monique, or Mona, as she was called back then, had their issues in high school, and Faye went so far as to actually rip up some of Monique's artwork. To me, as an artist, that's actually painful to contemplate."

Both Chip and Pamela nodded.

"More recently, Faye threw Monique out of her house because she was chatting up her husband Grant. I think we can rest assured that the flirting really happened because we've all seen Monique in action. She was a natural. Perhaps she couldn't stop herself."

"She didn't mean anything by it," Chip protested. "She was just being friendly."

"I think you're right that she didn't mean anything by it," Pamela agreed, "but some of the men and their wives or girlfriends didn't take it that way at all—Valerie and Frank, for instance."

"That's right. Also, we know that Faye seems to be laser-focused on Monique's pastels and how much they're worth. She's asked Pamela about them more than once. We don't know whether she's so interested because she thinks she can make money from them or because she wants to destroy them, although Monique's last words to Chip would tend to suggest it's the latter."

"My head is spinning," Chip said. "Why would Faye want to destroy Monique's artwork when she knows it's valuable? It doesn't make sense."

"No, it doesn't, but here's something that *does* make sense: Faye's been in Carrie's house, so she would have known where Betty and Carrie keep the keys to the rooms on the third floor."

"I had no idea," Pamela said. "How do you know that?"

"Because yesterday at the memorial service, Betty recognized Faye as one of the cleaning crew. She subbed on the crew from time to time. So, Faye could have been at the party in disguise and grabbed the key to the cupola. She could have texted or phoned Monique to meet her up there."

"Do you think she lured Monique up to the cupola to kill her?"

"Not necessarily, but maybe things got out of hand, and they quarreled. Anyway, the police should be able to confirm whether they were in contact by their examination of Monique's phone records. And one more thing: Faye showed up at the county coroner's office to ask about her belongings. That must mean she wants something, maybe Monique's diamond earrings, but the coroner told me that all of the jewelry Faye wore to the party was costume jewelry. Chip, you remember her earrings, don't you? They were huge, bright and shiny rhinestone chandeliers, not her dainty diamond studs."

"Right, I do remember. They were very flashy, hard to miss."

"Then there's the fact that Faye filed for probate: she wants something very badly, and, whatever it is, she doesn't trust Todd Whitman to give it to her, so she beat him to it. I think I'd better give Lieutenant Belmont a call. Granted, we have no real physical evidence, but there's plenty of circumstantial evidence pointing to Faye. The police could at least bring her in for questioning."

Chapter 34

I called the police station and asked for Lieutenant Belmont, but the dispatcher informed me that he was out of town, so I asked to speak to Dave. When I learned that he was also "out of town," I called Dawn to find out where the two officers were.

"They went to a community policing seminar in Phoenix," Dawn said. "It started yesterday and wraps up sometime this afternoon."

"Do you have any idea what time they'll be back in Lonesome Valley?"

"Nothing too definite. I hope Dave's back in time so that he's home when the trick-or-treaters start coming around the neighborhood. We had some nasty pranks on our block last year, and he was planning to patrol around and head off any trouble this evening."

"OK, I guess I'll get in touch later, then."

After Dawn and I wrapped up our conversation, Pamela said, "I could leave a message on Bill's cell phone, but maybe it could wait until tomorrow. As you indicated, everything we know is just circumstantial, and it doesn't sound to me as though it's enough for an arrest, so they might be questioning her, but even so, probably not on Halloween night."

"That's true," I agreed. "I suppose it could wait until tomorrow. Faye's not going anywhere, and if she *is* the murderer, I doubt that she'd be a danger to anyone else because I don't think there's any doubt that only Monique was the target. It's not like Faye's a serial killer."

We probably would have spent the rest of our shift speculating about Faye and Monique, but an older white-haired couple, both artists, came into the gallery to inquire about the possibility of joining the Roadrunner, so we were occupied with giving them the run-down. When one o'clock rolled around and our replacements arrived, both Chip and I left the gallery. He was headed to the pizza parlor, and I intended to go home, but I couldn't stop thinking about Faye.

Before I started my car, I searched the county recorder's site to find out whether Faye and Grant Stanhope owned a house in Lonesome Valley. From Faye's meltdown when she'd come into the gallery to tell her cousin that she couldn't stay with her anymore, I knew Faye and Grant lived in a house, not an apartment, but if they rented, I'd be out of luck and I'd have to look elsewhere to try to find their address.

Fortunately, their street and house number popped right up when I searched their names. Resolving to pay Faye a little visit, I entered her address into my GPS app. I'd have to think of some pretext for showing up on her doorstep out of the blue so that she'd talk to me. Then perhaps I could steer the conversation to the night of the party, ask her where she was that evening, and observe her reaction. Of course, Faye might figure out that I suspected her or she might not even be at home, but I couldn't shake the feeling of being drawn to her house.

I called Belle to tell her I had an errand to run and to make sure she was able to keep Laddie longer. If not, I'd go straight home. Belle told me to take my time, though. As usual, our two canines were having a great time playing together, but Belle told me they were beginning to tire and she was sure they'd take an afternoon nap.

Assured that Laddie was fine, I started the car and pulled away from the curb, I tried to think of plausible excuses to visit Faye. She knew I was a member of the Roadrunner, and she was obsessed with Monique's pastels, so I settled on a plan to tell her that she might want to move the pastels to a commercial, rather than a co-op, gallery for display after the end of the year, when Faye's paid membership at the Roadrunner would lapse. I could tell her that I would be able to put her in touch with the owner of the gallery in Scottsdale, where I was represented and where my paintings would be featured in a spring show. Confident that I could sound credible when discussing such a plan, I drove to Faye's house, a small Southwestern-style residence on a quiet side street.

I parked across the street from Faye's house. A few other cars were parked on the street, too, but I didn't see anybody outside. Of course, the absence of outdoor activity wasn't too unusual. School-age children would be in class, and probably most of their parents worked, so they wouldn't be home in the early afternoon, either. Although retirees might be, several bikes and toys visible in the front and side yards told me this was a neighborhood occupied primarily by younger people.

Before I got out of the car, I decided to try Lieutenant Belmont once more, just in case he'd be returning to Lonesome Valley early. This time, I called his cell phone directly, but my call went straight to voicemail, and I left a brief message, informing him of my suspicions about Faye.

Just in case he had returned early and wasn't answering his cell phone, I called the police station. When the dispatcher told me the lieutenant was out of town, I asked to be connected to Sergeant Boyd. I told myself that it might be a mistake to talk to him, but if I alerted him to the possibility that Faye had killed her cousin, he might pay attention.

I was wrong. After giving Boyd a rundown on the reasons for my suspicions, I was disappointed to hear him discount the information I'd provided him.

"Well, could you please at least remind Lieutenant Belmont that I called and need to speak to him?" I asked in frustration.

"Uh, huh," he replied. He couldn't have sounded more bored if he'd tried.

"Please. It's very important. I'm at Faye's house now, and I'm going to try to talk to her." I said before ending the call. I didn't wait for an answer since the sergeant had been so non-responsive during our brief conversation. No wonder Lieutenant Belmont had become irritated with the newbie on more than one occasion.

With a shrug, I grabbed my bag, crossed the street, and knocked on Faye's front door. It hadn't occurred to me earlier that her husband Grant might be home since I knew truck drivers didn't exactly work bankers' hours, but, if he were, I could still use my ruse to speak with Faye, and he'd be none the wiser.

My knocking hadn't brought Faye to the door, so I pressed the doorbell and waited a few minutes before realizing that she must not be home. I turned and started back down the sidewalk, but I'd taken only a few steps before I heard a shrill scream coming from the backyard.

If the neighborhood had been a busy one, people would have heard it and come running to see what was the matter, but there wasn't a soul stirring. Cautiously, I crept around the side of the house. The screaming had stopped, but I could hear a voice as I peeked around the back corner of the small residence to see Faye cowering on the patio. She stepped back and tripped when she ran into the single back porch step, and she pitched over sideways, landing painfully on her elbow.

Meantime, the man holding the gun on her never wavered.

Chapter 35

"Are you crazy?" Faye yelled. "Get that thing out of my face, and help me up!"

For someone who was being held at gunpoint, Faye was coming on strong, but she must have been scared when he pulled the gun on her; otherwise, she wouldn't have screamed.

"Get *yourself* up," he growled, waving the gun around. Even though he had his back turned to me, I could now tell that it was Todd Whitman. "We need to talk."

"I don't have anything to say to you."

"You'd *better* have."

"Or what? You're going to shoot me, right here in my own backyard?" Faye asked defiantly.

"Will you shut up? Just tell me where it is, and I'll be on my way. And you're not going to say a word to anybody, or else."

Faye sneered, but her lower lip was trembling. I realized she was frightened but was trying to put on a show for Todd in hopes he'd back down.

"I don't know what you're talking about," Faye said, stumbling to her feet and rubbing her elbow.

"Sure you do. Don't give me that."

"No. I really don't. If you're looking for the pastels that she left in her room when I kicked her out, they're not here anymore. I burned them."

"Now who's the crazy one? I don't care about the artwork. Do whatever you want with it."

Faye stared at him, and, in that moment, I knew she didn't have the slightest idea what Todd was after, and neither did I.

"Her ring," he continued, "Where's her ring?"

"I wouldn't know." Faye replied. "She was wearing it the day I kicked her out, and that's the last time I saw her alive."

"I don't believe you. She wasn't wearing it when she went over the balcony."

Faye's eyes narrowed. "How would you know?"

Todd didn't answer.

"You creep! You pushed her!"

Todd ignored Faye's outburst. "I want that pink diamond. The cops don't have it; neither does the coroner. And I'm certain it's not in the safe at the Resort because I already checked with the desk clerk there. You're the only one Monique trusted, even though you two didn't get along, so I know you know. That's why you filed for probate, so you could get your hands on it."

"No, it isn't," Faye protested. "I wanted her pastels because I felt guilty that I'd burned some of them. They meant a lot to her."

"I don't buy your lame excuses for a minute. You want that diamond as much as I do."

"You're wrong. I didn't even know her ring was a diamond," Faye wailed.

"Where's that ring? Tell me, or you're going to regret it."

As tears slid down her cheeks, Faye began to tremble. Todd sounded like he meant business, and he still had his gun trained on her.

If I could just find a way to distract him, maybe Faye could make a run for it. Otherwise, the situation was likely to deteriorate rapidly. Todd had already killed one person; he probably wouldn't hesitate to make it two.

I looked around for something to throw at Todd. Like most of the yards of residents of Lonesome Valley, Faye and Grant's contained some pebbles and larger rocks, which the locals used for desert land-scaping. Unfortunately, only very small stones were tucked around the perimeter of their house. I backed up a bit and found a few larger rocks at the base of a small palm tree. I grabbed a couple and crept back to my hiding place at the corner of the house.

Taking a deep breath, I held one of the rocks firmly and moved my arm backwards in preparation to pitch it at Todd. I'd never excelled at baseball, and I was far from confident that I could hit my mark, but I had to try. I hurled the rock as hard as I could.

The years hadn't improved my pitching arm, and the rock sailed past Todd without making contact. He whirled around, and even though I tried to quickly duck back behind the corner of the house as he started to turn, I didn't make it in time.

He pointed the weapon at me.

"Stop right there, or I'll shoot," he shouted.

I froze.

"Come here," he commanded, gesturing with the gun.

I walked slowly toward him. Meanwhile, Faye had taken advantage of the distraction and edged her way onto the back stoop. She hadn't made any noise, and Todd was too busy watching me to notice that she'd moved.

Once she reached the back door, she didn't bother trying to be quiet anymore. She yanked it open, went inside, and slammed it shut.

Todd and I could hear her jamming the bolt into place.

"I'm calling the cops!" she yelled.

Todd rushed to the back door and yanked on it with his left hand while still training his gun on me, which he held in his right hand. When the door didn't budge, he put his left shoulder into it, but only succeeding in hurting himself.

He let loose with a string of foul language that would have made a sailor blush.

"You might as well surrender," I told him. "The police will be here in a minute."

He laughed. "In this hick town? I'll take them half an hour just to find the house."

"Wrong."

Todd and I both turned to see Sergeant Boyd, who'd taken a stance and held his own gun with both hands pointed squarely at Todd. Before Todd had a chance to react, we heard the wail of sirens.

I realized that Boyd had come to Faye's because of my call earlier, the call I'd thought he'd ignored.

"Drop it! Backup's on the way," he said confidently, although it was impossible that he'd been made aware of Faye's call for help.

"OK," Todd said and started to lower his gun. As soon as he agreed to Boyd's demand, Boyd relaxed his stance. Letting down his guard hadn't been the best idea he'd ever had because Todd took advantage of the sergeant's lapse by grabbing me by the hair.

I struggled to dislodge his hand, but he managed to get his left arm around my neck before pointing his gun at my temple.

"*You* drop it!" Todd shouted. "Or you won't like the consequences."

Boyd hesitated. It looked as though he might be about to throw down his police special when we heard the sirens getting very loud. The shrill sound cut off as we heard tires screeching, and Boyd resumed his stance. Four uniformed officers came running up behind him. As they took in the situation and saw that the sergeant had his gun drawn, they drew theirs, too.

"You're outnumbered. Drop your weapon!" Boyd yelled.

Todd responded by tightening his arm around my neck and pressing the muzzle of his gun to my face.

Chapter 36

I'd never been so scared in my life. Todd was cornered and desperate, but instead of surrendering, he'd chosen to use me as a human shield in his stand-off with the police.

"Now let's be reasonable, Mr. Whitman," Boyd said. "Let the lady go."

"No! She's coming with me! Get out of my way!"

When Todd jerked me forward, he moved his gun slightly so that it was no longer pressing on my skin, but it was still only inches away. If he discharged it, I'd never survive. My whole life literally flashed before me in a few seconds, and, despite some problems and heartaches along the way, I did not want it to end now.

As Todd roughly dragged me, he began swinging his gun around, pointing it from one officer to another as he forced me to move forward. The police were holding their positions, rather than moving back to let Todd through their ranks.

"I mean business," he yelled as he fired a shot over their heads.

When he fired, he loosened his grip on me, and I stumbled, caught myself, and landed on one knee. The ground was rock hard, and my knee felt like it was on fire, but I didn't waste a second.

I grabbed Todd's calf with both hands and yanked with all my might. This time I didn't miss my mark. He fell to the ground, and his gun flew out of his hand as he landed. He scrambled for the weapon, but the five police officers swarmed him before he could reach it.

One of the uniformed officers secured the weapon while another clapped Todd into handcuffs and a third officer began reading him his rights.

Sergeant Boyd helped me up, and I dusted myself off.

"Are you all right, Amanda?" he asked. "I can call an ambulance."

"No need; I'm not in shock, just a bruised knee I think," I responded, surprised that he remembered my name. "Todd as much as admitted that he pushed Monique to her death. Faye and I both heard him."

"Faye? The woman you suspected?"

"Yes, obviously I was wrong. I came here to speak to her, and that's when I saw Todd threatening her with that gun of his. He didn't notice me at first, but when I threw a rock at him, Faye was able to run into the house and call for help."

"I wondered why I had backup without ever calling for it."

"Thank you for paying attention to me when I called earlier. That *is* why you came here, isn't it?"

"Yes. I got to thinking about what you said; it made sense, so I decided I'd better check it out for myself."

He pointed to the back stoop, where Faye was standing. She must have been watching the scene from the house, and now that Todd was safely in police custody, she'd emerged. "I take it that's Faye over there."

"Yes."

"I've questioned a lot of people in this case, but she wasn't one of them. Wait till Lieutenant Belmont hears about this!"

"Boyd!" There was no mistaking that gruff voice. We looked around to see the lieutenant and Dave coming around the corner of the house.

"Yessir," the sergeant snapped to attention as though he were in the military.

"Would you care to explain?" Lieutenant Belmont growled.

"We arrested Todd Whitman," Boyd said.

"I can see that. What are the charges?"

Boyd gulped before firmly asserting, "Aggravated assault with a deadly weapon and murder."

"Todd killed Monique," I piped up, "and he was threatening Faye with his gun when I got here because he wanted Monique's ring and he thought Faye knew where it was. She was able to run inside after I distracted him."

Boyd interrupted me to say, "He was holding his gun to Amanda's head when we got here. She tripped him up after he fired a shot, and that's when we got him."

The lieutenant looked at me and shook his head. "Don't you think you've had enough of playing Nancy Drew? You could have been killed."

"I know. You don't have to remind me." Although the day wasn't especially cool, I'd begun to tremble, and a light-headed feeling was coming over me again.

Dave reached out to steady me. "Let's go over here, where you can sit down." Dave held onto me while he guided me to a lawn chair on Faye's patio. When Faye saw how badly I was shaking, she went inside and came back out with a blanket, which she tucked around me.

"Thanks for saving my bacon. I'd be a goner if it wasn't for you. Why *did* you come here, anyway?"

"Oh, uh, I was going to tell you about the Ian Adams Gallery in Scottsdale, where I exhibit some of my art. I thought maybe you might want to move Monique's pastels there after the first of the year."

Sergeant Boyd and Lieutenant Belmont rolled their eyes, but, luckily, Faye missed seeing their reaction to my fib.

"That's nice of you."

Her statement earned another discreet eye roll from the detectives.

"I suppose you heard me tell Todd that I burned some of Monique's artwork." she continued. "It was spiteful, I know, but I was so mad at her for flirting with Grant. When I heard she was going to that party at Carrie's, I had second thoughts. After all, she was my only living relative, and we quarreled a lot, but we always made up. That's why I texted her to meet me in the cupola the night of the party; I figured it would be a private place to talk, but I never made it there that night. My car wouldn't start. By the time I got the battery replaced, it was too late, so I texted Monique to meet me the next day. I never heard her again, though."

Faye stepped back abruptly and looked at me with concern.

"Honey, I'm going to make you a nice hot cup of tea. You're shaking all over."

"What's this about a ring?" Lieutenant Belmont asked after Faye went inside.

"Todd mentioned a pink diamond. Monique was wearing a pink ring the evening I first met her when she returned to the Roadrunner. I thought it was a pink topaz, but it sounds as though it's actually a pink diamond."

Boyd let out a low whistle. Lieutenant Belmont raised an eyebrow, and we all stared at the police department's newest sergeant.

"Pink diamonds can be worth a fortune," Boyd explained. "I read about a rare one that sold at Sotheby's for nearly thirty-five million dollars. Of course, they're not all quite *that* valuable, but I bet the one Todd was looking for is probably worth several million."

"But why would he push Monique over the balcony railing?" Dave asked. "He claimed he wanted to marry her. Why not just wait until they were married? Then, he could have talked her into selling it and gotten his hands on the money."

"That *is* strange. He certainly didn't act like he was short on funds. He was staying at the Resort, which costs hundreds of dollars a day, and he paid for Monique's memorial service. The video he had produced to show at the service couldn't have come cheap, either," I said.

We could only speculate on Todd's actions that afternoon, but the mystery of why he did what he did was revealed a few days later when Brooks himself told me that when Todd had extended his stay at the Resort after Monique's death, the desk clerk had failed to run his credit card again, and it turned out that it had been maxed out during his stay.

Another revelation from Brooks explained the reason that Todd hadn't been able to locate Monique's pink diamond ring in the safe at the Resort. Although he'd convinced the desk clerk to check for it in the hotel safe, he'd never asked Brooks about it. Brooks told me he'd insisted on keeping it for her in his own personal safe before she left for Carrie's party.

Over the next several weeks, more news about Todd surfaced, and we learned that, although he lived a lavish lifestyle, he'd run up huge gambling debts, and he'd been counting on marrying Monique, selling the diamond, and getting access to the funds so that he could bail himself out of his financial problems.

He claimed Monique's fall from the balcony was an accident, but the county district attorney wasn't buying his story, and Todd was charged with voluntary manslaughter, since the D.A. didn't think that Todd had planned to kill her. He figured Todd and Monique had quarreled, he'd become angry, and pushed her. However, more charges were added since Todd had not only threatened both Faye and me but had also taken a shot at the police officers. To top it off, he was charged with issuing a bad check when the funeral home complained that the one that Todd had written to pay for Monique's memorial service had bounced.

All those revelations came later, though.

After I gratefully downed the cup of tea Faye brought me, I stopped shivering and I felt more than ready to head for home, although I wasn't looking forward to the lecture Emma would surely give me when she learned that I'd been held at gunpoint.

Still, it certainly beat the alternative.

Chapter 37

When I arrived at Belle's house to pick up Laddie, I told her what had happened, and she was as astonished as I had been that my trip to Faye's had ended with Todd's arrest.

"A lot of clues pointed to Faye as the culprit," I told Belle, who'd urged me to put my feet up and try to relax for a little while before going home.

Mr. Big hopped onto my lap, and, to my surprise, Laddie followed. Laddie didn't usually get up on the furniture, although he slept on my bed at night, but I'd never expressly forbidden him to do so; he'd just never seemed interested in being a lap dog before.

Belle and I both laughed as the two dogs vied for my attention. Mr. Big soon tired of the competition, so he jumped down and ran to Belle, who obliged him by picking him up. Laddie snuggled even closer to me as I petted him.

"He seems to know I'm still shaken from my ordeal," I said.

"He sure does. He's a sensitive boy," Belle replied. "But what am I thinking? Let me fix you a nice hot cup of tea."

"That's exactly what Faye said to me after it was over! And I have to say, it did help calm me down a bit, but I think I'm about tea-ed out for now."

"How about some chocolate cake then?" Belle suggested, as she gently set Mr. Big down on the floor.

"Now you're talking!"

When Laddie and Mr. Big heard Belle rattling around in the kitchen, they wasted no time in following her. Their efforts were rewarded when she gave them each a tuna fish tidbit.

Wagging their tails, they trailed her back to the living room, where she served me a lovely slice of chocolate cake and took charge of the dogs while I ate it.

"That was wonderful, Belle. Thank you. I guess I'd better be going. Emma should be home soon, and I'll have to face the music."

"She'll be upset that you were in danger, of course, but there was really no way you could have anticipated that Todd would be at Faye's house with a gun."

"That's true. All the clues seemed to point to her. I thought maybe she'd let something slip if I spoke with her. I had no idea that what I thought was a topaz in Monique's ring was really a pink diamond or that Todd must have desperately wanted money."

"Well, you were getting close. Who knows what would have happened if you hadn't interrupted Todd?"

"Of if the cops hadn't shown up when they did." I shuddered. I knew the trauma of this day would be with me for a long time.

Emma must have thought the same because she wasn't nearly as hard on me as I'd feared. After some tears from both of us and a big hug, she suggested that we should get ready for the Halloween trick-or-treaters.

Pivoting from the events of the afternoon, I dressed in my Victorian bathing costume, and Emma put on a green satin skating outfit that she'd worn to a party last year. We stood together while she took a selfie of us as Laddie and Mona Lisa looked on.

"Now it's your turn," Emma told Mona Lisa, picking up the purring kitty.

She carefully set a little gray crocheted hat on top of Mona Lisa's head.

"What a darling cap with the pink-lined ears! Now she looks like a mouse."

"I bet she'd rather catch a mouse than be one," Emma giggled. "Do you think you can hold her still while I take her picture?"

"Sure."

I managed to hold onto my calico cat just long enough for Emma to get a picture. Then, with a loud "meow," she was off to the top of her kitty tree, where she managed to shake the crocheted hat off and push it over the side to the floor.

"I guess we know what she thought about that," I said, hurrying to pick it off the floor before Laddie had a chance to pounce on it and whip it around in his mouth as he did with his soft toy. "Time to get your costume on, Laddie."

He held still while I put his lion outfit on him and adjusted it. He knew he was handsome boy, and he pranced around the room, perfectly happy to be dressed up for Halloween.

Emma coaxed Mona Lisa down from her kitty tree and popped the mouse hat back on her head before the kitty realized what was happening. Then, Emma snapped a few pictures of all four of us in our costumes before the first trick-or-treaters arrived.

As soon as they knocked on the door, Mona Lisa took off for the bedroom, where she'd likely spend the rest of the evening under my bed.

As the groups of children came, we all went to the door and surprised them with our costumes while complimenting them on theirs. Laddie was the hit of the evening, though. He knew most of the kids from around the neighborhood, and they got a big kick out of seeing him dressed like a lion.

After a couple of hours handing out candy, we had a lull.

"Do you think we have enough treats to last?" Emma asked, looking at the large bowl I'd set out. "It's getting a little low."

"There's plenty more in the cupboard. I'll grab another bag."

While I was in the kitchen, the doorbell rang. Most of the little ghosts and goblins had knocked on the door and chanted "trick or treat," but, this time, there was only the doorbell, and whoever was ringing it kept it up, over and over.

"What in the world. . . ."

"Maybe you'd better get it," Emma said, with a Mona Lisa smile.

I pulled open the door, and there stood Brian, dressed in cowboy get-up.

"Wahl, howdy pahtner," he drawled. "Thought I'd mosey on over."

"Brian!"

"Happy Halloween," he said, twirling me around and planting a big kiss on my mouth while Emma and Laddie took in the scene.

Of course, Laddie couldn't contain himself for too long, and he began racing around us in circles.

"I think he wants to say 'Happy Halloween,' too," Emma said.

"Is that what you want, Laddie?" I asked.

He emitted two short woofs as he bounced around in joy.

"All right, then," I agreed. "A very Happy Halloween to all of us!"

Thanksgiving Dinner Sub

Amanda and her friends occasionally indulge in a Thanksgiving Dinner Sub from the Coffee Klatsch, next door to the Roadrunner. It's a meal on a bun! Although perfect to prepare with your leftovers from Thanksgiving dinner, this sandwich can be enjoyed any time of the year.

Ingredients

six-inch sub roll
mayonnaise
roasted turkey
cranberry sauce
sage dressing
mashed potatoes
chicken or turkey gravy

Directions

Spread mayonnaise on the bottom half of the sub roll and then pile on turkey, cranberry sauce, dressing, and mashed potatoes. Drizzle gravy over the potatoes and crown the sandwich with the top half of the sub roll. Cut the sub into two pieces in the middle. The sandwich can be quite thick, depending on the quantity of ingredients you use (there really is no set amount), so you may need to eat it with the aid of a knife and fork.

Artichoke Quiche

Belle told Amanda she cheated by using a ready-to-bake pie crust for her new quiche recipe, but Amanda assured her that using the ready-made crust was well worth it since it saved a lot of time.

Ingredients

1 frozen ready-to-bake deep dish pie crust

1 cup uncooked rice (this doesn't go in the custard mix, but it's used to weight the crust so that it doesn't buckle while baking)

1 teaspoon olive oil

2 minced garlic cloves

1/3 cup chopped purple onion

14 ounce can artichoke hearts

½ cup sun-dried Julienne-style tomatoes (in bag, not in jar with oil)

1 cup shredded Monterey Jack cheese

4 large eggs

1 cup half and half

½ teaspoon salt

½ teaspoon black pepper

Directions

Preheat the oven to temperature suggested for the ready-to-bake frozen pie crust. Line the pie crust with parchment paper. Spread one cup of uncooked rice evenly in the bottom of the pie crust to prevent it from buckling during baking. Bake the suggested time. Remove the pie crust. Before filling, make sure to discard the rice. Adjust oven temperature to 350 degrees. In a non-stick pan, add a teaspoon of olive oil, minced garlic, and chopped onion and sauté. Set aside. Place the eggs in a bowl and use a wire whisk to beat them. Add the half and half, salt, and pepper. Layer the artichokes, sun-dried tomatoes, and garlic-onion mix in the pie shell and sprinkle cheese on top. Pour the egg mixture over the cheese. Set the quiche on a cookie sheet and bake at 350 degrees for 45 – 60 minutes. The top should be browned and the center set before you remove the quiche from the oven. Allow the quiche to cool on a rack for ten minutes before serving.

Makes 6 servings

Crunchy Sweet Potato and Pomegranate Casserole

Here's a hearty fall dish, perfect for cool autumn days. After Amanda moved to Arizona, where pomegranates are plentiful, she began using them in recipes, and Belle showed her how to remove the arils. If you want to try this recipe and don't know how to cut and seed a pomegranate, consult one of the many YouTube video demos for techniques.

Ingredients

two 15-ounce cans of sweet potatoes
one 21-ounce can of apple pie filling
¾ cup pomegranate arils
½ cup toasted pecans

Directions

Seed a pomegranate to remove the arils. If you've used water in the process, drain them and place on paper towels to remove excess water. Preheat the oven to 350 degrees. Spread the pecans on a baking sheet covered with parchment paper and roast for about 10 minutes, turning after 5 minutes. Watch them carefully so that they do not burn. Drain the sweet potatoes. Combine the sweet potatoes and the apple pie filling in a small casserole dish (1.5-quart dish or 8" x 8" baking pan). Bake for 45 minutes at 350 degrees. Just before serving, sprinkle the pomegranate arils on the top and then the toasted pecans.

Pumpkin Pancakes with Cream Cheese Syrup

Amanda enjoyed pumpkin pancakes with cream cheese syrup at the Lonesome Valley Resort. Here's her version of the recipe.

Syrup Ingredients

4 ounces cream cheese (room temperature)

1/3 cup light corn syrup

1/3 cup powdered sugar

1 tablespoon (or more, as needed) milk

Pancake Ingredients

2 cups all-purpose baking mix

¼ cup brown sugar

1 cup milk

2 large eggs

1 cup pumpkin puree

2 teaspoons pumpkin pie spice

Directions

Set the cream cheese out about an hour before you plan on making the pancakes with syrup so that it will soften. In a mixing bowl, beat the cream cheese until it's smooth. Add the corn syrup and beat. Add the powdered sugar and beat. Mix in one tablespoon of milk and mix well so that the syrup won't be too thick. You can add more milk if necessary to make the syrup pourable.

Set the syrup aside and prepare the pancake batter. Beat milk, eggs, and the pumpkin puree in a medium mixing bowl. Add the dry ingredients and mix. Lightly coat a large nonstick skillet with oil or butter and set it on medium heat. Pour about one-quarter cup of the pancake batter into the skillet for each pancake. When several bubbles have burst on top of the pancake, flip it and continue cooking until done. Serve warm with the cream cheese syrup.

Makes about 12 pancakes.

About the Author

USA Today bestselling author Paula Darnell is a former college instructor who has a Bachelor of Arts in English degree from the University of Iowa and a Master of Arts in English degree from the University of Nevada, Reno. *Halloween Hue-Dunit* is the fifth book in her Fine Art Mystery series. She's also the author of the DIY Diva Mystery series and *The Six-Week Solution*, a historical mystery set in Reno. She resides in Las Vegas with her husband Gary and their golden retriever Lindsey Lou.

VISIT HER WEBSITE

pauladarnellauthor.com

Books by Paula Darnell

DIY Diva Mystery Series

Death by Association
Death by Design
Death by Proxy

Fine Art Mystery Series

Artistic License to Kill
Vanished into Plein Air
Hemlock for the Holidays
Killer Art in the Park
Halloween Hue-Dunit

Historical Mystery

The Six-Week Solution

www.ingramcontent.com/pod-product-compliance
Lightning Source LLC
Chambersburg PA
CBHW061543210726
48287CB00006B/2056